REAL UGLY

HARD ROCK ROOTS

Book One

To Karen, Mrs. Turner Campbell xx

C.M. STUNICH

SARIAN ROYAL

These are real people with real problems. This is real life, and it's real fucked up.

BOOKS BY C.M. STUNICH

for the world's coolest cats, in no particular order. you may not have fur, but you still rock the alley. Jennifer Martinez, Leanne Jacobson, and Marlena Fein.

thanks for being wicked awesome.

CHAPTER 1
❧ NAOMI KNOX ❧

There's a metamorphosis happening right before my eyes. I'm watching a devil shed its skin, shrink its horns and grow wings. The dark haze in the air is lifting, banished by the bright lights of the stage. Even metaphorically, a trick like that is hard to pull off. I'm impressed. Or I would be if I didn't hate the asshole so much.

"He looks like a fucking angel," I whisper as I sip my beer.

"What?" Blair shouts, cupping her hand around my ear. I swipe some hair away from my face and lean over, so that she can hear me above the booming of the bass. It pounds down through the wood of the stage, into the concrete, and across the floor where it catches on the

rubber soles of my boots and ricochets up through my bones. If I close my eyes, I can see it tainting my blood, forcing my heart to pump faster and faster, until I feel dizzy from the beautiful poison in the air. The phrase *slaying the crowd* wasn't made up off the top of someone's head; if the fucks on stage do it right, it really does feel like the music is killing you softly.

"Turner Campbell," I yell back at her, my lips brushing against the small, black plugs in her earlobes. "He looks like a fucking angel up there." Blair leans back and raises one pierced brow at me. Her blue eyes say that I'm full of shit. I take another sip of cool, cool amber and watch as she turns her heart shaped face to the stage. Her gaze rakes Turner from head to toe and then slides across the heaving, thumping crowd, landing right back on me.

"A fallen angel," she shouts. Pauses. "*Maybe.*"

I shrug and ignore her pointed stare, watching Turner as he moves across the stage, lights glistening off the blue-black highlights in his hair and making him look like he has a damn halo on his head. His brown eyes scan the crowd, catching on faces and holding them as he purrs into the microphone and caresses it like he fucking *owns* it. I bet every bitch in here can practically feel his hands on her body, taste his tongue in her mouth. *What am I shitting myself for? They've probably all had a nice,*

big slice of the real thing anyway. Let's just say that Turner's reputation proceeds him.

Devil.

I have to remember that he's not just a devil, but *The Devil.*

I take another sip of beer and try to focus on something else – the crowd of people clusterfucking at the bar, the mosh pit up front, Blair's white feather eyelashes. Nothing works. My gaze finds Turner Campbell again and stays there, focusing primarily on his lips and the words that tumble out of them.

"What the hell did you do to leave me broken, barren, and bleeding? What gave you the fucking right?" Turner sucks in a massive lungful of air, blowing his hot breath across the microphone and breaking my heart with a single gasp. I'm not alone. The crowd starts to hum, men and women alike pulsing with the heat and the energy of the song. *Goddamn, that's good,* I think as I allow myself to sink against the cool concrete of the back wall. *Doubt those lyrics are his though. Fucking hypocrite.* Just yesterday I walked in on Turner fucking a roadie over a PA speaker. When he saw me, he just pulled out and left the girl there with her panties around her ankles. She cried for a half a fucking hour. *Devil.* I want to hate him, but it's really hard from down here. I like it better when I'm backstage, when I can look at him hitting on groupies

and roadies, watch him running his fingers across the lips of a dozen girls in a dozen cities. It's a lot easier to hate him that way. *How am I going to make it through six months of this?*

I finish my beer and push away from the wall, dropping the empty bottle on the edge of the bar before sneaking out a side door. My hands slide across a collage of torn stickers and scribbled Sharpie as I heave the heavy metal out of my way, snatching one last glance before I go at the lead singer of Indecency. Sweat slides down the tattoos on his neck and soaks into the fabric of his black T-shirt. Ironically, it's one of ours. *Amatory Riot.* I doubt he even really knows who we are. I bet one his roadie bitches dressed him this morning.

I drop the door shut behind me, not caring that the sound of it slamming is like a gunshot in the still air outside the Pound. I'm glad our set is over because it would be hard to follow an act like that. No matter what I think of Turner, his band is good. I guess they'd have to be since they're the headliners. Still …

I put a cigarette between my lips and light up. The tangy coastal air feels good against my moist skin and the breeze smells like salt, waking me from the buzzed trance I was nursing and thrusting me back into the real world. Not always a good thing.

"Hey, Naomi," a voice calls out from the end of the

alley. I don't turn my head because there's only one person I've ever met that sounds like a demonic version of Mickey Mouse. "Hayden got drunk and vomited all over the bathroom. There's like three inches of fucking puke in there." Wren pauses next to me and tucks his skinny hands into the front pockets of his acid washed jeans. "It smells like tequila and it's making me sick." I take a drag on my cigarette and close my eyes. The music from inside is drifting through the walls and poking the bare skin on my arms like a chorus of needles. I sigh and flick my smoke to the grimy cement.

"So clean it up," I tell him as I crush the butt to ashes with the toe of my stiletto boot. "I'm tired of being Hayden's bitch." Wren watches me, but doesn't say anything else. He knows I'll do it. That I'll walk in there and pick our lead singer up off the floor, wipe her down and strip her naked, put her to bed and tell her a goddamn fairy tale. I'm no stranger to cleaning up Hayden's messes. I just have to get my head in the right place before I do it. Wren shifts his weight to the side and continues to stare. "Fuck, don't just stand there and stare at me. You know I'll friggin' do it. Gimme a minute, why don't you?"

I turn away and start down the alley, back towards the front where bouncers in black shirts wait, passing around a silver flask and sharing a joint. They know me, so they

don't say anything, just watch as I step into their circle and reach out my hand. Both items make their way to me quickly.

"I love your shit, Knox," says a man with bright blue eyes and a tattoo of a dragon curling up his left arm. I swig some of the alcohol from the flask. *Ugh. Cheap whiskey.* I wipe my hand across my mouth and hand it the person standing next to me.

"My shit?" I ask as I pinch the joint between my fingers and slide it into my mouth. I take a nice, long drag and wait for the smoke to fill my lungs and cloud my brain. I can't look at Hayden if I don't get fucked up first. Ever since that day, the sight of her makes me sick to my stomach. *God, I hate that bitch.*

"Your music. It's good shit." I blow white smoke into the air and smile with tight lips.

"If you ever call my music *shit* again," I say as I pass the joint to dragon-boy. "I will kick your fucking ass to the curb."

I make out with dragon-boy for awhile and stop just short

of second base. He seems pretty pissed off, but I'm not a fucking whore, and I'm just not that into sex right now. My head feels light and fluffy, like it's been stuffed with cotton, and I'm having trouble walking. I have to stop in the alley and sit on the dirty cement, so I can take my stilettos off. It isn't easy to navigate in four inch heels, especially with the alcohol and the THC roiling around inside of me.

I throw the leather boots over my arm and stumble back to the bus, fully expecting to find Hayden right where Wren left her – drunk and drowning in puke. When I open the door, I get a whole other story.

"Right there, baby," Hayden is growling, hands curled around the edge of the countertop. Behind her, Turner Campbell is thrusting his dick like he's in a fucking marathon or something, gripping her skinny hips with white knuckles and squeezing his eyes shut tight. He doesn't even look up when I ascend the creaky steps.

"What the fuck, Hayden?" I ask, but she's so out of it that she doesn't hear me. Turner does, I can tell, but he doesn't respond either. Doesn't stop. The wet sound of their bodies sliding together makes my stomach twist dangerously. Vomit climbs my throat, but I swallow it back. "Hey, motherfucker," I snarl, forgetting instantly about that angelic presence I saw on stage. It was all a trick of the light, a nice, fat slice of show business that he

shoved down everybody's throat – including mine. He's back to being a devil again. How could I have ever forgotten? After what he did to me before, I should slit his freaking throat and toss him out the window, let the stray dogs in the alley finish him off. "Get off of her! She's fucking wasted, you asshole." I throw my boots on the floor and move forward, putting one hand on Turner's chest and shoving him back. He stumbles and hits the cabinets with a grunt, sliding to the floor with his dick hanging out of his pants and his shirt bunched up around his midsection. Bits of spiderweb peek out at me from under the black fabric of his tee, crawling down and wrapping his cock. He's even got tattoos on the damn thing. You'd think I'd have noticed that before, but I guess I was too busy getting my cherry popped to think about much else.

"What the hell?" he moans, putting a hand to his head and rubbing at his forehead with fingers wrapped in ink. When Turner pushes his hair back, the edges of star tattoos wink at me from his hairline. He's obviously trashed as shit, too, and doesn't make even a halfhearted attempt to stand up on his own. I roll my eyes and ignore him, throwing an arm around Hayden's waist as she tilts to the side and threatens to topple over. I don't have much love for the bitch, but if she dies, Amatory Riot is pretty much screwed sideways. It would be a sort of

love/hate thing for me if she were to fall and crack her head open.

"Goddamn it, Lee," I growl at her as I drag her boney ass across the floor and kick open the doors to the sleeper section of the bus. Hayden is still covered in puke, so I force her to stumble into the shower and let her slump the floor. I turn the water on *cold*.

"Shit!" she shouts, her voice trailing off into a moan. Hayden's head slams into the tile wall and she starts to sob. "What are you doing to me?" she cries as I step back and run a hand through my hair. Blair is glancing at me from her position on the floor of the second bathroom, a sponge in one hand and a bucket in the other. Looks like most of the vomit is gone.

"Thanks," I say, but she's already shaking her head, tossing the sponge into the bucket and sitting up. The knees of her jeans are soaked through and her white tee is stained with something questionable. She looks pissed.

"Don't thank me, Naomi," she says as she stands up and leans against the door frame, popping a cig in her mouth as she relaxes against the wood. "This is Hayden's oversight, Hayden's tequila, Hayden's mess." Blair takes a drag and throws the cigarette into the bucket. "Stop taking responsibility for her shit." I don't respond because Blair doesn't know what happened between Hayden and me. If she did, she'd understand. I don't like

her thinking I'm Hayden's lapdog, but what can I do about it? The bitch has shit on me for days. *God, I am so super fucked.* I shrug and turn around, ignoring the grunts of irritation from the bunk on my right.

"Fuck you, Wren," I snarl as I move past him and take note of the other bunk. *Looks like Kash is in tonight. What a surprise.* Kash is having some kind of fucked up affair with two chicks – the driver for Indecency and the bassist from Terre Haute. He almost never spends the night on our bus.

I pause in the doorway and stare down at Turner Campbell and his flaccid dick.

"Get up, Turner," I bark at him, moving forward and poking his leg with my toes. "And get the fuck out. Go." He moans, but he doesn't move. I think he's even drooling on his shoulder. *Pathetic. If your groupies could only see you now.* "Turner. Get the hell off of my bus."

"What is your problem?" he whispers, sharp lips barely moving with the words. He sounds lucid enough, but he looks like shit. I put my hands on my hips and try to make a judgment call. It isn't easy with my head swimming like the Northern Pacific. I could go and grab one of Turner's band members, see if they'd come and get him, but I dread going on that bus in the middle of the night. That is, if their stupid ass bodyguard will even let

me pass. Besides, the odds of finding anybody in that band that isn't trashed at this hour are pretty slim.

"Stand up," I command as I watch his hand travel between his legs, snap the empty condom off and toss it onto our carpet. My lips curl into a sneer, and I end up grabbing his arm and dragging him up off the floor. His skin is hot to the touch and sweaty as hell. *Please don't OD on my bus, you stupid fuck,* I think as I struggle to pull the world's biggest asshole to his feet. I don't like the man, by any means, but if he dies then I'm guessing they'll probably cancel the rest of the tour, and that would be a big ass, fucking drag for me and my band. Guess the least I can do is prevent him from drowning in his own vomit tonight. If keeping him on his back and wiping dribble from his chin will keep my dream afloat then the rest of the world be damned, I'll fucking do it. I can always take pictures as backup and sell them to the tabloids if everything goes to hell.

"Shit, Naomi," he growls, and I drop his arm like it's poisoned. Turner falls to his knees in front of me and leans against the wall, head hanging down between my legs and hands flat on the floor. "Just leave me alone. Leave me the fuck alone."

I stare down at the back of his neck, at the inky paw prints that climb his spine and disappear into his dark hair.

"What did you just say?"

Turner groans and lets himself slump fully against the cabinet before he opens his mouth and vomits right past that beautiful, little tongue ring of his. *What a friggin' douche,* I think, and then before I can stop it, my brain adds, *that remembers your name.* Hearing the three syllables of my earthly monicker pass through his lips was nothing short of a shot to the back of the head. I didn't even think that he knew the name of my band, let alone mine personally.

"Ah, shit," Blair says from behind me, making me jump as she sidles around me and stares down at the growing stain on the carpet. "This is great. Just great. Now we get to drive all the way to San Diego with the smell of Turner Campbell's puke." She smiles at me with tight lips. "But hey, what's new, right? I feel like we're eternally in this fucker's shadow." She kicks Turner with the pointed toe of her red heel. "Still think he looks like an angel?"

I sigh.

"Just shut up, Blair, and help me pick him up."

She frowns at me and tucks some of her blonde and black hair behind an ear while I dig my arms under Turner's pits and try to drag him to his feet.

"And what, pray tell, are we going to do with him once we get him up?" she asks as she bends down and

joins me, tits practically spilling out the top of the tight corset she's got on. All three of us groan as we shift Turner's comatose body between us, leaving his legs dangling on the ground like perverted puppet masters in the world's worst marionette show.

"Just put him in my bed," I say as I ignore another pointed stare from Blair.

"He's totally out, Mi. I doubt he could even get it up right now."

"Blair, seriously?" I ask her as we dump him on the bottom bunk and shove his legs up onto my black comforter. "I'm not even going to respond to that," I tell her as I hear a whimper from the bathroom and suddenly remember that I've left Hayden in an ice old shower. *Oops.* Blair and I exchange a look, and she sighs.

"Yes, I will clean up Campbell's puke as long as you don't start apologizing for him, too."

"Fuck him," I say.

"Good girl," she tells me and spins away on her heel while I retreat back to the bathroom and switch off the water. Hayden is curled into a fetal position, sobbing, and while that's not unusual, it's kind of disturbing to watch.

I grab a towel from under the sink and throw it to her. It hits her in the face and falls to the floor. Hayden lets out a wail that makes my teeth hurt, and I suddenly regret

grabbing the bitch before she fell. *Should've let her crack her head wide open,* I think as I step forward and start to strip her down. She doesn't protest, just flops around limply and lets me tear off her expensive, designer clothing that's supposed to scream 'I'm a rebel!', but instead just makes her look like a fucking tool.

"Come on," I say to her as I grab her by the wrists. Don't need any help lifting this bitch. She weighs, like, maybe eighty freaking pounds. "You stupid, anorexic, motherfucker," I snort as I drag Hayden into the hallway and practically shove her onto the bunk opposite Turner. As soon as her wet head hits the pillow, she starts to snore. I watch her for a moment and turn away, catching a glimpse of Turner's shuttered eyelids and gently parted lips. Believe it or not, he looks like a fucking angel again. I flick one of his lip piercings with my fingernails and move back into the kitchen/living room area with a sigh. The pot and the whiskey have already abandoned me and left me alone with nothing but stark, white reality. "Is it wrong to hate someone so much it hurts?" I ask Blair as she sprays the rug with some sort of organic cleaner that I just know isn't going to work. The last one she used was made out of tropical fruit and smelled like bubble gum; the piss stain on the hallway floor is still there. Enough said.

"Are you talking about Hayden or Turner?" Blair asks

as we both look up and watch our driver/roadie/personal bitch, Spencer Harmon, step into the RV. She's got two armfuls of groceries and a wrinkled lip.

"God, what is that smell?" she asks as she sets the bags down and watches Blair go back to work, leather clad ass up in the air flashing a three inch line of butt crack. If I was into chicks, it'd be kind of hot.

"Turner Campbell's leftovers," I say as I pop in a cigarette and smoke it with short, sharp puffs like it's a cigar or some shit. I watch with disgust as goose bumps spring up all over Spencer's arms and legs. Her full lips part gently and her dark lashes flutter.

"Turner Campbell was here?" she whispers, and I can't hold back the scowl that crosses my face. I shouldn't get so annoyed at the girl. I mean, she's only one of thousands who've fallen for that man's charisma. *Myself included.*

"Yeah, and he's trashed as shit. I walked in on him and Hayden fucking."

"Hey," Blair snaps as she sits up and pushes her bucket away, wiping an arm across her forehead. "I had to watch the whole thing happen and even *listen* to it." I ignore her, and I don't ask why she didn't put a stop to it. Nobody stands up to Hayden except for me, and even then, it's questionable. Same thing goes for Turner Campbell, but not because he's scary like Hayden. He's

just a god of the stage. He can do no wrong. I resist the urge to spit on the floor. It's already bad enough down there.

"Oh," Spencer says, but the wonder in her brown eyes doesn't die and her skin prickles and crackles like it's been lit on fire. She removes the groceries like she's in a daze, pulling out healthy snacks like celery and carrots and broccoli that only she and Blair will eat. I can only hope there's something in there that's loaded up with carbs and sugar. "What time did he leave?"

"He didn't," I say, gesturing over my shoulder with my chin. I stab my cigarette out in an ashtray that's overflowing onto the table and shrug nonchalantly. "He's so fucked up that he couldn't stand. I put him in my bed." Spencer's eyes open wide, and I have to cut her off before she can even offer. "No, I'll sleep on the couch," I say and I can practically see her heart bursting out of her chest at the thought of spending the night within touching distance of Mr. Campbell. As irritating as the whole scene is, I'm glad because there is no way in shit that I would spend another night anywhere near that man. The first was bad enough. *Jesus, Naomi, that was six years ago. Get the fuck over it. You know he doesn't remember, so why should you?*

"Look at you," Blair says as she stands up, pulling the bucket along with her. "All empathetic and shit. Good

for you, Naomi."

"Fuck you," I say as I give her the finger, grab a can of beer from the fridge and curl up on the black sofa that sits across from the door. I pop the top and nurse my drink while I watch Spencer finish putting away the groceries. When she's done, she just stands there and wrings her hands like she's about to walk into an interview or something. "He doesn't bite," I say and immediately wish I hadn't. *Oh, wait. Yes, yes, he does.* I suck down half my can as I watch her watching me.

"You really do hate him, don't you?" she asks, and I shrug nonchalantly. But when I speak, I'm dead fucking serious. I raise my eyes to meet Spencer's.

"More than anyone else on this godforsaken earth."

CHAPTER 2
✥ TURNER CAMPBELL ✥

Shit. I wake up in a cloudy haze with a pounding head and a churning stomach. *Where the fuck am I?* I wonder as I slam my forehead into the bunk above me and struggle to sit up without retching all over the goddamn place. Across from me, there's a girl with brunette hair sprawled out naked. I look her up and down, but she's skinny as fuck and not very attractive, at least not to me. I stare at her for awhile trying to figure out if I should know her, but the face doesn't ring any bells, so I stand up and take stock of the situation. I feel like shit, but hey, things have been worse. At least I didn't wake up in an alley or in some stranger's car on the way to friggin' Mexico. *I touch my stomach with gentle fingers. And it*

doesn't look like anybody cut out your organs while you were passed out. It's a good day for you, Turner.

I eye the bathroom for a moment before deciding I've probably done enough damage here for one day. I can retch at my own place. Better to get out of here before any of these bitches wake up and start accusing me of shit. I've already got one pending suit because some whore told the cops I pissed on her. *Fucking slut.*

I wipe my hand across my mouth and grimace. The skin around my lips is crusted with dried puke and my whole throat feels like it's been washed in a bath of acid. Not good. I've got another show tomorrow, and the last thing I need is to screw my voice up. If I cancel another set, my manager is going to flip the fuck out. I should really fire that son of a bitch.

I stumble out into the kitchen and look around for the fridge. You wouldn't think it would be that hard to find, but my vision is kind of blurry and my head is spinning like crazy, so I don't see the stainless gleaming at me in the moonlight. Not until I've tried half of the other cabinets. They do crap like that in these fancy as fuck buses. Hide fridges in cabinets. I hate that shit.

I yank the door open harder than I probably should and jump when a groan sounds from behind me. A quick glance over the shoulder reveals a girl curled up in the rectangle of bright as fuck light that's coming from the

fridge. She shifts her body and turns away mumbling something incoherent, and a light goes off somewhere in my clogged skull. *I know this girl,* I think as I turn back to the contents of the fridge with a pinched brow. There are cans of freaking tomato juice stacked side by side with beer. I take the stupid choice and grab a brown bottle before I turn around and pop the top off on the bottom of the counter.

You know every girl, asshole, I tell myself as I step forward and stare down at her shadowed face. It's too dark, and I'm too whacked out to see much, but I reach out anyway and brush some of the pale hair from her forehead. The movement reveals a pretty face and moist lips, but not much else. A memory niggles at the edges of my skull, but when I try to reach for it, it pulls away and leaves me empty. Doesn't bother me much. Happens all the fucking time. I shrug and turn around, dropping my half empty beer onto the counter before I leave, pulling open the door to the bus and squinting at the quiet darkness around me.

A man looms up out of nowhere and gets in my face.

"Who the fuck are you?" he asks, breathing hot against my cheek before I reach out with both hands and shove him back. The man grunts and stumbles hard, coming up swinging. That only lasts so long as it takes him to catch my gaze. "Ah," he says, and I watch with a

smug smile as the fight leaves him and his arms fall to his sides. "Turner, sorry. Didn't know it was you." The dude steps out of my way and pauses like he thinks I'm going to move past. Instead, I reach into my pocket and pull out a cigarette.

"Must be nice having so much pussy onboard," I say as I cup my hand around the cig and light up. The wind's starting to blow pretty hard out here. "So much cock on my bus that I wake up every morning choking on dick." *God, I wish I could get some blow.* "Got any coke?" I ask real quick. Guy looks like he's about to burst the veins in his neck. The dude, whoever he is, snorts, but he doesn't leave. I think he wants to move past me, but knows better than to try. "Know anybody I could score some off of?"

"No." Real short and sharp. This guy doesn't like me. I smile.

"What's your name?" I ask as I flick the butt of my cigarette to the ground and run my tongue over my lips.

"Dax."

"No last name, Dax? You're a real rock star, aren't you?" I laugh and move away without waiting for him to answer. I don't really give a shit what he has to say. Some guy from a B-list band isn't my problem. These pretty boy drummers are a dime a dozen.

I wind my way through the trailers and buses, bracing

myself by putting my hands up against the sides. The world is fuzzy around the edges and spinning like a fucking tilt-a-whatever. I just need to find my bus and climb into bed. Shouldn't be hard to find anyway. It's the biggest, nicest, one of them all.

Just as it should be.

"Turner!"

"Aw, fuck me," I growl as I continue on and ignore the pound of footsteps behind me. I'm not in the frame of mind to deal with Milo's shit today. "Leave me alone."

"Things aren't like they used to be, Turner. This isn't the eighties. Rock stars have to do more than just drink and fuck. You've got an image to maintain."

"Yeah?" I pull my phone out of my pocket, snap an Instagram shot of my face and post it every-fucking-where. *Status: Late night out, bitches. Enjoy.* I reach into my pants, snap another shot and post that, too. From behind me, Milo groans.

"You're going to get banned for that," he says as I grab the handle to the door and pull it open. I slam it in his face and lock it, not caring that he has nowhere else to go. He can hang out on his iPad and do PR work, fix the mess I just made. And then he can get me a cup of coffee in the morning. I'm sure he'll be just fine. Guys like Milo don't need sleep. They get all their energy from sucking the life out of others.

I kick beer cans and boxes aside, cursing as I stumble towards the back. All the bunks are full, including mine. At first I think it's Treyjan, and I get all pissy, but then I pull the covers back and find myself with a nice, little surprise.

"Well, hello there, beautiful," I say as I examine the half-naked girl curled up in my sheets. She raises her head and smiles at me.

"Your bandmates let me in. I hope … I hope that's okay." I look the girl up and down again, and a grin curls the edges of my lips.

"Oh yeah, sexy," I tell her as I kick off my boots and slip under the covers. "That's more than okay with me."

Milo wakes me up in the morning by thrusting a cup of coffee under my nose. The smell of it makes me sick to my stomach.

"Get that out of my fucking face," I snap as my eyes water, and I struggle to sit up without bumping my head on the top bunk. When I put my hand out to brace myself, I come up against a bit of soft, warm flesh. It's a

girl, of course. It always is. I've got one in my bed every night, same as the fucking pillow under my head. Unfortunately for her, the pillow's the only one that gets to stay. The blonde smiles up at me, and I smile back.

"Good morning," she whispers, snuggling closer to my arm.

"Good morning, sunshine," I say as I lean down and lock lips with hers. All the while, I'm aware that Milo is standing there clutching my coffee in tight fingers and frowning. I consider fucking the girl again, just to screw with his head, but at second glance, she isn't so pretty in the morning light. I pull away and keep smiling.

"I don't mean to rush your good-byes, but we have to leave. We're on a tight schedule here, Turner. All unauthorized personnel need to get off the bus." Both the girl and me ignore my manager's whining.

"I had a good time last night," she says, nibbling her lower lip and running her fingers up my arm. When she reaches under the blankets, I stop her with a gentle grip around the wrist. Lifting her hand to my mouth, I kiss her knuckles softly and look out from under my lashes. Think it's a chick trick? Guess you've never fucking tried it. Women love long eyelashes.

"Me, too, babe," I say as I press her hand against her chest and notch my smile up to a grin. "If I hook you up with a backstage page, you think maybe you can catch

me at another show?" She nods vigorously and brushes some bleach blonde behind her ear. I tap her under the chin and wink, turning away before she can get another word out and slapping my feet on the gleaming wood floor of the bus.

"Hook her up with some swag," I tell Milo as I grab the coffee and make my way over to the bathroom. There's someone inside, but I don't bother to ask who it is. I just kick open the door and take a sip of my coffee. The glass door splits open and a wet face glares out at me. "Morning Treyjan," I say as I glance over my shoulder and watch as Milo hands the girl from last night a white robe, throwing me a narrow eyed glare while he goes about cleaning up after me. I have a hard time feeling sympathy for him. It's what I fucking pay him for, isn't?

"Have a good time last night?" Treyjan says as he slides the door closed and goes back to washing his hair. "Sure as fuck sounded like it to the rest of us." I lean against the door frame, not caring that I'm still buck friggin' naked. Let 'em all get an eyeful and enjoy. I take another sip of the coffee. It isn't exactly doing much for my hangover, but at least it'll wake me up. I check to make sure the girl's far enough way that I can speak freely.

"I guess it was alright," I tell him as I step back and

use my foot to pull open the drawer beneath my bunk. I fish out a T-shirt and a pair of jeans, throwing them on quick and finishing my coffee in a single gulp. "Where'd you find this one?" I toss my garbage into the can next to the toilet. It hits the rim and bounces off, but I don't bother to pick it up. I pay someone to do that, too.

"When you didn't show up last night, we made a bet to see which chick would wait around the longest looking for you. Found her by the merch table flirting with Jason."

"Should've left her there, too," I say and we both laugh. "And hurry your fat ass up, you fucking diva. The rest of us could use a shower, too. Especially Josh."

"Hey, fuck you, Turner," Josh says as he pushes past me and disappears into the second bathroom, slamming the door behind him. I ignore him. He's always a bitch in the morning. Not as bad as Milo though.

"Excuse me?" my manager asks as I step into the kitchen and open the fridge. I am fucking starving. I start to rummage through the crap inside, looking for something I can actually eat. Most of it is complete shit, and I end up closing it without finding a damn thing. I pull a cigarette out of my front pocket and stick it in my mouth.

"Can't we get some fucking food on this damn bus? Am I supposed to friggin' starve to death?" I shove past

Milo and reach for the door handle. "I'm going to Denny's. Try not to leave without me."

"Turner!" Milo screams as I snag my boots on my way out and hit the dust barefoot. "We have to be in San Diego by eight o'clock tonight. If we don't leave in the next half hour, we're not going to make it." Fucking Christ. That man is worse than my mother.

"Then buy me some goddamn food." I pause and drop my boots to the ground, lighting my cigarette before I step into them. I don't bother to tie up the laces. "Get something on that bus other than red licorice and fucking chia seeds, whatever the hell those are."

Whatever Milo says next, I ignore, moving through the buses and trailers with my cig hanging out of my mouth and my phone in my hand. There's quite a load of messages on my Facebook page. Guess my fans liked last night's post. I smile and search for a Denny's, hoping to fuck that there's one within walking distance. If I don't get something to eat soon, I'm done for.

I'm looking down, so I'm not paying attention to where I'm going. Doesn't matter anyway. When people see me coming, they get out of my way.

"Hey!" a girl shouts as our shoulders slam together and my cigarette topples out of my mouth. "Watch where you're fucking going!" A crumpled ball of leather slams into my chest before I get the chance to process that the

chick standing in front of me is the girl from the bus last night, the one on the couch. *Holy fuck me. She looks even better in the daylight.* She's tall, fucking got legs for days, and her tits are practically falling out the top of an asymmetrical tee that's cut up and hanging in long strips over her bare belly. Skin like porcelain, orange-brown eyes that bite, and swollen lips. *Hell to the fuck yeah. She's exactly my type.* My irritation at having her bump into me dissipates right away, and I switch on the charm.

"Hey, baby, do I know you from somewhere?" I shake out the crumpled leather as she scowls at me and realize with a start that it's actually my jacket. Must've left it on her bus last night. I wonder if we fucked. If we did, then it's a memory I'm sad to forget.

"Yeah, last night when I cleaned your puke off my carpet and pulled your dick out of my friend. Hey, next time you decide to screw a drunk chick, make sure she's sober enough to remember her own name. Can you do that for me, Turner?" I lick my lips and shake out the jacket, tossing it over my shoulder with a scowl of my own. Hot as this chick is, nobody talks to me like that. If I've ever fought for anything in my life, it's the right to be respected. Even a tight body and a dangerous scowl can't change that.

"Hey, if I touched your friend, it's because she wanted me to." I snap my fingers and lean in close. "Oh yeah,

and it's none of your damn business." Hands come out quick and hit my chest, knocking me back a step. Mostly from surprise. She isn't as tough as she thinks.

"Next time you pass out on my bus, I take payment from you in the form of diseased body parts." She waves her hand at my dick and then tries to turn away. My fingers on her shoulder spin her around and this time, she hits me right in the face.

"You fucking bitch," I snarl as she stands her ground and stares me down. "I could have you kicked off the tour for that shit. Or thrown in jail. Who the hell do you think you are?" The woman raises her chin and takes a deep breath while the wind teases her dirty blonde hair around her soft face. She's acting fierce, but I can see right through her. This chick is vulnerable, half ready to crack. Wonder if I could help her along a little? Broken souls are my specialty.

"My name is Naomi Knox," she says and then takes a step closer to me, so close that the toes of our shoes touch and her breasts brush up against my chest. Almost immediately, my cock springs to attention and gets hard as a fucking rock, expanding along the length of my thigh and pressing against the tight fabric of my jeans. *Fuck that hurts. Guess this my penance for wearing girls' pants.* "And I'm not afraid of you, Turner Campbell, so fuck off."

She spins on her heel and smacks me across the cheek with her hair. As she moves away, I see something in her face. I don't know what it is, but her words trigger something else in me. I know I've met this girl before, and I'm not going to rest until I figure out where.

CHAPTER 3
❧ NAOMI KNOX ❧

Shit.

Even sober, Turner Campbell still recognizes me. My face at least, if no longer my name. As hard as that is to believe. I saw it in his eyes. I knew taking that jacket over there was a mistake. I should've just thrown it away. *Then why didn't you, Naomi? Did you actually want to see him?* I shake my head and run my fingers through my hair. Watching him onstage last night wasn't the smartest move to make. It almost made me forget, and I can never, ever let that happen.

"Thanks for last night," Hayden says as I walk past. She's leaning against the side of the bus smoking a joint and wearing a purple jersey that does nothing to cover her

small tits or her lacy panties. She doesn't even care that half the roadies have hard-ons, and the other half are trying to melt her with laser-eyed glares. I snatch it from her lips and throw it to the ground, pulling the door to the bus open and hopping up the steps. "Hey!" she shouts, way too slow on the uptake. She drops to her knees and digs around the shrubs for it.

"It's seven o'clock in the morning, Hayden." She doesn't remember last night at all which is a fucking blessing. She'd either be furious about fucking Turner or ecstatic. Frankly, I'm not sure which and that scares me. Nobody bothers to fill her in.

I pause in the kitchen and stare at Kash and Wren slumped over bowls of cereal, milk dribbling from their chins as they scoop soggy bits into their mouths and focus on the wall with twin zombie stares. Looks like I'm the only one who didn't have a good time last night.

"Was he as pleasant this morning as he was last night?" Dax asks, scooting past me and diving into the cabinets above the stove. I stare at his shirtless back and try to focus on the words etched along his shoulder blades. *Born to Bleed.* I lean against the counter and close my eyes. I guess there's no sense in pretending, but I do it anyway.

"Who?" Dax snorts and slams the cabinets closed, taking a bag of pretzels along with him as he spins to face

me.

"Turner. Who else? You know, I had no idea how easy it could be to hate someone. What a fucking entitled asshole. He thinks because he dropped a couple hundred thousand albums that he owns the world?" I shrug and pretend I'm not interested in this conversation. I can't be. I don't have time for this. I've got better shit to do. Like write new music. God knows I'm the only one that'll fucking do it.

I open my eyes and look up as Hayden stumbles onto the bus and glares at me, flipping me the bird before retreating into the back and collapsing onto her bunk. Hey, she can hate me all she wants, but I need her to sing tonight. And as long as I don't push her too far, our secret is safe. With a sigh, I push myself forward and head off in search of our manager. She's great at composing Tweets, starting threads, and blogging about us, but when it comes to real life shit like making sure we get to our next gig on time, eh. I could do a better job. I check the bunks in my search for her and come up empty-handed. All I end up finding is Blair jacking herself off which actually doesn't interest me much. She's a pretty girl and all, but I was born with this horrible affliction that leaves me attracted to men. Why haven't they invented a cure for that shit yet? Check the facts. It's the world's deadliest disease. I kid you not.

I slip out the front door and narrowly manage to miss an argument between the boys. Could be about politics, religion, or whose cock is the biggest. I don't fucking give a shit. All I know is that it's the last thing I want to get in the middle of. I'm in a bad friggin' mood today. *I knew this tour was a bad idea. Only two weeks on the road and you're already losing it. You thought keeping your distance would keep you safe? Hah. You were wrong, Naomi. Dead wrong.*

I pound down the steps and let my eyes sift through the crowd carefully. The parking lot's finally coming alive, drawing partiers out of the woodwork just in time for them to remember that they actually have jobs to do.

"Naomi." It's America. Good. Found without a search. I turn to face her and notice that her smart phone isn't glued to her face like usual. Immediately, I suspect that something's wrong and narrow my eyes.

"What?"

America pauses a few feet away from me and draws a tablet from her purse, sliding her fingernails across the screen without taking her gaze from mine.

"I've got some good news and some bad."

"Bad first," I spit, letting my eyelashes flutter closed for a moment. A cigarette makes it out of my pocket and into my mouth, crackling nice and pretty with hot, orange light. America watches it with unveiled disgust, but

doesn't lose her white-toothed smile. I stare at her, tearing her apart with my eyes, trying to figure out what would convince a Harvard grad to take up managing a rock band. I mean, it's not like the woman went all buck wild and dyed her blonde hair black, painted her nails with tiny skulls, and started sporting plaid minis. She still wears dark slacks and cream colored blouses, slicks her hair back into severe buns, and uses only neutral eye shadows. She looks and acts the part of a stuck up lawyer, but she isn't one. I mean, yeah, she passed the bar exam and all, but other than a brief internship, she's never practiced.

She stares right back at me and never flinches; the locks remain tight and the chains wrapped. Whatever secrets America is hiding will remain in the dark. Unlike mine, apparently.

"I got a little home movie sent to me last night. I was going to show you then, but when I got back to the bus, I found you in a bit of a sticky situation."

I blow smoke out and huff at her.

"Sticky situation? The only thing that was sticky was the cum Blair and I had to scrub off of the carpet. The shit that was going down wasn't mine." America blinks at me, but remains stoic. Her white, white skin glows with well placed spots of blush and the best moisturizer money can buy.

"Really? How odd then that I'd receive this the very same night that Turner Campbell made his debut on our bus."

The tablet is handed over to me, and I watch as I reach out and grab it with sure fingers. *Whatever this is, I can handle it. I can handle anything.*

I spin the screen around and watch the video.

Seconds later, I'm around the back of the bus throwing up.

I can handle anything. Anything except this.

My secret.

Well, one of them anyway.

"What are you thinking?" I ask America as we sit on the bus and sip coffee. We're over two hours behind schedule, but nobody can find Turner Campbell and much as I hate the stupid fuck, the circus can't leave without its ring leader. I'm kidding myself if I don't acknowledge that at least half of the fans that show up to our gigs are there not just for Indecency, but for the lead singer himself. He practically fucks them with his voice,

splits their souls in half and enslaves him. I hate him, yes, but I cannot, cannot, cannot deny that.

"What you really mean is, does this change anything?" America holds her mug in two hands and sips carefully, letting the Brazilian blend sit on the back of her tongue before she swallows. Her knuckles are bare except for a silver wedding band. America is single. I don't want to know what that means. "And no. It doesn't." She sets her cup down and drums her fingertips on the tabletop. "Not unless you want it to. This changes nothing for me."

"But you're a lawyer." Her lip curls, and I can tell that I've said something I shouldn't. Oh fucking well. What's new? "Shouldn't you be … I don't know. Calling the cops or something?"

America laughs, and it's dry as hell. As arid as the fucking desert we're getting ready to travel through. She clacks her pretty pearly whites together and scowls at me. It's the first time I've ever seen an expression like that on her face, and it throws me off.

"I can forgive a lot, Naomi. A lot. But don't act like you know me." America slams her palms on the table and stands up. Before I can even get a grip on the situation, she has her phone at her ear and is screaming something into it. I set my coffee down and lean back, crossing my arms over my chest.

Okay, Naomi, let's get the facts straight. America saw something that should have her turning your ass in, and instead, she's mad because you called her out for what she is. Or what she should be, I guess is the right way of phrasing it. Um, what the fuck?

"Why are we still here?" Hayden asks, sliding back the pocket door that separates the bunks from the kitchen. "Shouldn't we be on the way to San Francisco already?" I lean back and kick my boots up on the table.

"San Diego, sweetie. We're already in San Francisco." Hayden narrows her eyes at me and watches as I light another cigarette and put it in my mouth. It's the least horrible vice I have, so I embrace it. Two packs a day keeps the shrinks away. "Remember? We played The Pound last night."

"Don't talk to me like I'm an idiot, Naomi," she says, tucking some of her brown hair behind her ear and blinking at me through gobs of dark eyeliner. She's smeared so much across her blue eyes that she looks like a robber. In a lot of ways, she really is, so it suits her I decide.

"Why not? That's what you are, isn't it? Only seems fitting." I give her a tight-lipped smile and stand up, moving to the window to flick back the curtain. If Turner doesn't come back soon, I'm going to go after him myself, and God help me, he'll wish his return had been

voluntary.

A hand sweeps my hair back and lips kiss my ear with poisoned words.

"You're getting awfully arrogant these days, Naomi. Think you're good enough to play for God now?" I continue to smoke my cigarette and I don't pay Hayden any never mind. I know how far I can push the bitch, and I'm not there yet.

"Did you send it?" I ask her casually, curling my fingers around the counter. If she did, I'll know, no matter how she responds. A quick glance over my shoulder shows me Hayden pouting her lips in the reflection of the oven. She isn't even listening anymore.

Good.

Then it wasn't her.

Fucking question is then, who was it? Nobody knows but us, just me and the bitch herself. And America. And whoever sent it.

Fuck.

"We made it up, and we played it through, and our lives were never. The same. Again." Hayden sings the lyrics to our most popular song and, like with Turner, I almost forget for a moment why I hate her. Then I turn around and see her shaking her ass and grinding her crotch up and down the fridge door while she searches for a drink, and I remember nice and quick. *God, I wish you*

would just fucking disappear, I think as America returns from wherever it was that she went.

She looks at Hayden for a moment and the corner of her mouth twitches just so.

"Turner's back," she says with her toothy smile stuck back across her lips. "With his majesty's blessing, we can now get this show on the road. Oh, and Naomi?"

I put my cigarette out in a glass ash tray and look her right in the face.

"Yeah?"

"Earlier, I forgot to tell you the good news." America fetches a pair of sunglasses from her front pocket and slides them up her perfectly straight nose. "The charges against you have been dropped. Looks like you're going to get away with murder."

CHAPTER 4
&xTURNER CAMPBELL x&

Naomi Isabelle Knox. Lead guitarist for Amatory Riot. Twenty-three years old. Hot as hell. Mean as sin.

I ask around; I get answers. What can I say? I have a face that's hard to resist. I spend the majority of the drive stalking her online, scoping out pictures on her band's website, raiding their Facebook page, scanning their blog. Naomi herself doesn't have an online presence for shit. All the info I've got on her is generic and unhelpful. I *know* that we've met before, and I'm determined to find out where. Don't know why I'm so obsessed with it. Maybe I'm losing it one fucking binge at a time, but that's okay. Live fast and die young, right? I want to leave a beautiful corpse.

I stuff my phone into the pocket of my jeans and stand up, slipping out from behind the table and making my way to the back where there's a small sofa and not much else. Hey, it's nice, but it's still a fucking bus. Might be a long way from the yellow piece of shit I used to ride to school, but that doesn't mean it's a friggin' mansion.

Ronnie is laying on his back, shirtless, sleeping away a hangover that makes my migraine look easy. He's been really into dropping acid lately, so I figure that's probably it.

"Hey bitch." I poke him with my boot. Ain't no way I'm touching that motherfucker. Let's just say that Ronnie isn't as discerning as little old me. Turner Campbell never forgets to bring balloons to the party, if you catch my drift. Ronnie … well, let's just say that half his fucking check goes to child support. The asshole has like, four kids or some shit.

He groans and turns away from me, burying his face in the red leather cushions, probably drooling all fucking over them, too.

"Get the fuck up," I command him, planting my hands on my hips. If you need answers about someone on the tour, just ask Ronnie. He's either fucked them, shared drugs with them, or had a fight with them. Probably all three. Ronnie's bisexual, so he makes sure to canvass the entire traveling party from roadies to managers to

guitarists.

"Leave me alone, fucker," he snarls as he bats his hands at some imaginary someone above his head. I kick his ass, literally. The scenery is fading to black outside and I can tell from Milo's anxiety attacks that we're almost to San Diego. The closer we get to our destination city, the more often he freaks out. Sometimes it seems like Milo Terrabotti has more issues than the rest of the band combined. Either that or the straight-edge little bitch's refusal to self-medicate isn't as pretty a practice as it is a thought.

"I need some dirt on a chick I met this morning," I tell him, hoping to grab his attention. Ronnie gossips worse than my eighty year old auntie. "Something about her has got under my skin and I'm itching for a little info here. Think you can snap yourself out of it long enough to tell me her story?" I smile as Ronnie sits up and runs his hand over his pale face. "Besides, you know we've got another show tonight, right?"

"Another?" he groans as he leans back and lets his mouth hang open wide, flashing me silver fillings. The stubble on his chin and cheeks crawls with shadows as lights flicker up and over us before disappearing into the night.

"Yeah, man," I say as I pull out a cigarette and light up real quick. "That's why they call it a tour, you know?

You travel around; you play music. Or are you too fucked up to remember that we're chasing a dream here?" Ronnie snorts and snaps his lips shut.

"Your dream, maybe," he tells me as he fishes out a joint and holds his hand out for a light. "Whatever it was I was after, is long gone now." He breathes deep and sighs, slinging his arms up along the back of the sofa, resting his grungy boots up on the table. If Milo saw this, he'd have a friggin' fit. Don't know why he cares so much anyhow; it's my fucking bus. "So, what's this mystery chick's name?" Ronnie lets his shadowed lids flutter closed, and a smile teases the edges of his lips. "And why the hell are you so interested in her? Last time you were this into a woman, you were trying to get the manager of Heartstrings Records to book us." A harsh laugh escapes my throat as I lean back against the door frame and pull a drag on my cig. "You must be crap in bed because as soon as she banged you, she was up and running like her life depended on it." Ronnie chuckles and opens his brown eyes. His pupils are so big they look almost black and kind of creepy, surrounded by shots of red veins that seem to pulse in the changing light. Normally, I'd blame that on the drugs, but this time, I think it has more to do with his past than anything else. Poor bastard.

"Hey, I showed her a good time that night. It was her

fucking mistake to leave her phone on the nightstand. Her husband called, and I answered." I shrug and brush off the past with a wave of my hand. I don't like to live in the what's been; I'd rather live in the now. The what's been wasn't all that great to me, and the now's been like some kind of fucked up fairytale. I sing; I sell records; I own the fucking world. The one thing I always wanted, I've got: respect.

Except from that girl.

Even thinking of her now is getting my blood hot and my fingers tight. I squeeze my cigarette hard and try not to let her get to me. It's hard though; I can still feel the sting of her palm against my cheek, see the disdain in her eyes. I grind the cherry of my cig into a glass ashtray and cross my arms over my chest.

"Naomi Knox," I say, and I watch as Ronnie's face registers the name. His mouth twitches and he scratches at the snake tattoos that crawl out of his shirt and around his neck.

"Huh." Just that one word. Now I'm even more intrigued. Ronnie's staring out the window with a wistful expression, letting his joint dangle from his lips while he thinks. His *Terre Haute* tee is stained with sweat, and I know it's just a matter of time before Milo bursts in here and starts shouting about appearances and image and all that crap. Me, I've already showered and done my hair,

applied a slash eyeliner around my eyes, and slipped into a black tee with a bleeding heart on the front. I've got on a new pair of jeans and a custom pair of hi-tops in solid black with our band logo on the side. Ronnie might not have a problem going onstage looking like he just stepped out of his double wide, but I do. I already lived a major part of my life doing just that. I've got money now, and fame, and respect, and I want to look the part. "Yeah, I know a little about Naomi Knox."

"A little?" I ask, leaning forward a bit. I feel like a kid sitting around a fucking campfire, waiting for a ghost story or some shit. I get pissed off all over again and lean back with a scowl. Ronnie smirks at me.

"Damn, Turner. You really are all wrapped up in this, huh? Something happen that I should know about it?"

"Do you know something or not?" I snap at him, feeling these little lines of fire open up in my veins. My blood gets hot, and I have to squeeze my fists tight to keep from getting angry again. The more I think about it, the more pissed off I get, and the last thing I need to be doing right now is starting some kind of shit with another band.

"Cool your jets, Turner. I said I know a little." He pauses and smokes for a minute before continuing. "I'm guessing you already know the basics, so I'll skip right to the good stuff." Ronnie smiles. "Naomi Knox is your

typical disgruntled foster kid. She doesn't have any family, blood or otherwise living, and she started playing guitar when was thirteen. She's a big fan of Monster energy drinks, and she won't fuck anybody on tour – not a manager, a roadie, or even a fellow musician." Ronnie pauses and pulls the joint from his mouth with one hand while he tugs on a black plug in his ear with the other. "That's not to say she's a vestal virgin or anything like that. I've seen her bring people back to her bus." Ronnie pauses again and a grin splits his face. "Not like you though, Turner," he amends. "Nobody's as a big a fucking whore as you."

"Hey, thanks for nothing," I tell him, flicking some cigarette ash at his face before I start back towards the front and bump into Milo. He looks me up and down, and I raise my brows at him. Guess he decides that I look okay and doesn't start any shit, scooting back, so I can slide past him.

Well, fuck. I feel like I know even less than I did when I started. I wanted a full history on this girl, and I got a smattering of useless fucking facts. Fine. That's fine.

A smile breaks my lips as I glance out the window and see the welcome sign for San Diego. Time for me to do a little digging. When I'm done with this girl, she won't even know what hit her.

I pull out my phone and dial a number.

CHAPTER 5
❧ NAOMI KNOX ❧

As we roll into San Diego, I get a phone call.

I grab a quick glance at the screen and see that the number's blocked. Not a good sign. I reject the call and slip it back into my pocket.

A notebook lies open in front of me, filled with scribbled, black drawings of wings and crying faces, swaying trees, and grinning demons. Whenever I can't write, I draw. Someday, maybe when I finally escape from Hayden's shadow, I'd like to draw our own cover art. I look up at the bitch in question and send her a silent *fuck you*. She's got on another of her Hot Topic outfits today – a black corset with buckles and a pair of designer jeans that came pre-ripped. I want to tear her red stilettos

off her feet and stab her in one of her too blue eyes.

"Got anything yet?" she asks me, like I'm some sort of lyrical machine. Hayden likes to play front woman and bask in the glory of masturbating boys and jealous women, but she doesn't do shit for this band. I mean, I'm sure her time is so much better spent taking topless photos for Tin Dolls Magazine, but it would be nice if she actually contributed something other than her tits and her voice.

"No." I don't justify her actions by saying anything aloud. Seems like Hayden will go out of her way to piss me off. Whenever I've voiced my displeasure, she seems to get worse, so I've learned to keep (most) of my thoughts to myself. I drum my fingers on the table and pull my phone out when I get another call from the mystery number. Reject, again. I slam the screen down on my notebook and slide my hands over my face.

"Are we there yet?" Dax asks, appearing in the kitchen dressed only in a pair of boxer shorts and a sheen of droplets from the shower. Hayden watches him like a hungry lioness and licks her lip, but he ignore her.

"Thirty-two minutes and counting," America says without ever pausing in her frenzied texting spree. "Get dressed and be ready to go. Thanks to Mr. Campbell, we're running horribly late. We'll be lucky if the venue even lets us play our set."

I sigh and pick up my pen, brushing ink across the blue-lined pages. Pen and paper are so much more inspirational than electronics. I find it unbelievable that anybody gets anything creative done on a computer. I like to cross words out and draw arrows and kiss the page; I like to feel the words under my fingertips, pressed so hard into the paper that they've let deep grooves. I think the day handwriting disappears for good is the day humanity is really and truly fucked.

Another call comes through from the mystery number, and I answer it.

"Who the fuck are you and what the hell do you want?"

"Wow. Your foster parents never taught you any manners?" My heart catches in my chest.

"Who the fuck is this?" I repeat, my pulse racing in my veins. America's pried her eyes from her iPhone and is staring at me with a frown on her face. She can tell something's wrong. Luckily, everybody else in my band is a fucking idiot and doesn't notice the sweat on my forehead or the quiver in my voice. The other person on the line has to be the one that sent me that video. Who else would call and answer with such a cryptic message?

There's a long span of silence and then a deep exhalation of breath, like whoever's on the other end of this line is pissed off.

"This is Turner Campbell."

Oh.

I frown, but at least my heart can stop trying to explode from my chest. America stands up and moves over to me, holding out her hand for the phone, but I shake my head. *I got this,* I mouth at her.

"How the hell did you get my number?" I snarl at him, feeling horribly violated. I want nothing to do with this man, haven't wanted anything to do with him since he left me after taking my virginity. And the worst part of it all? He doesn't even remember doing it. I feel sick. What's that old saying? Hell hath no fury like a woman scorned? I used to worship Indecency, Turner in particular, and now … even the sound of his voice gives me chills.

"The Internet is a beautiful, beautiful thing," he responds, and I can hear the smile taking over his voice. This man flips moods like a picture book. One page, a smiley face, the next, a frown. That's dangerous fucking behavior. Besides, the deeper he digs, the more likely he is to hit things long buried. I want my secrets kept six feet under, thank you very much.

"Leave me the fuck alone, you psycho stalker," I say and draw the attention of everyone on the bus. Hayden swoops in close and tries to listen while Blair gives me a sympathetic smile from across the room. I hear Turner scoff and then the call ends abruptly. A few seconds later,

it rings again, and I answer with a, "What, you didn't get it the first time? I said to fuck off." I swear to God, I can hear his jaw clenching, can practically see veins bulging out of his throat. I bet he's all red-faced and pissed, just like he was the night that he saved my life and fucked me both at the same time.

"I want to talk to you about something."

"That's what I have a manager for. Call her. Milo's got her number." I get ready to hang up again, but pause when Turner laughs. It's too cruel, and it makes my toes curl and my body heat up from below. I am so screwed if that little sound can get my pussy pulsing and thrumming like a good bass line. *I should be immune to this shit by now.*

"Oh, this isn't about music. This is personal. Come out for drinks with me after the show tonight." I frown and my body goes from hot to cold in a New York minute. I don't like the way he's talking to me. He's not asking; he's telling. I hate being told what to fucking do … I get enough of that from Hayden. But then, is he the one that sent the video? I mean, I can't outright go and ask him, but it would make sense based on the timing, especially if he knows more than he's letting on about what happened between him and me.

"Give me one good reason why I should go out for drinks at two in the fucking morning with some asswad

who cares more about his eyeliner than he does about the women he sleeps with?" The phone goes dead silent, and the only sound is Kash's laugher ringing out from behind the pocket door to the bunk beds. I bet he's just eating this shit up.

"You really are a frigid bitch, aren't you?" he asks me which just makes me want to go all buck friggin' wild and take his head off with my guitar. They don't call 'em axes for nothing. "Come out with me tonight." He pauses. "Or don't. Your choice. Hope you make the right one."

And then he hangs up on me and doesn't call back.

That son of a bitch.

I set my phone down with a trembling hand and try to puzzle out what's going. Either Turner's just being an asshole or he knows. Do I take a chance on that?

"Who was that?" Hayden asks, tossing her hair over one shoulder with a flick of her red fingernails. She smiles down at me with a wicked look that makes me stomach twist uncomfortably. No matter if Turner knows or not, Hayden does for sure, and I can never, ever forget that.

X X X

I stand on the right side of the stage and watch Terre Haute finishing up their set. They're good, but not good enough. I bet they won't last out the year. I pull my cigarette from my mouth and toss it into a nearby trash can. Not normally a good idea, but I'm not the only who's done it, so I figure it's alright.

My eyes dart around, searching for Turner with each flick across the room. I've been expecting him to come after me this entire time, but he hasn't set foot off that ostentatious fucking bus of his. I wonder what he's doing there, if he even cares that we're about to play in front of a few thousand people. Maybe that's small fucking beans to him now; I don't know, but what I do know is that if I see him before I go onstage, that I'm going to be wrecked. And I don't want to be. I don't like to get trashed until *after* I've played.

"Oh God, I'm so nervous," Hayden says, stretching her arms above her head and not looking at all like she's ever been nervous about anything. She says this before every show, no matter the size of the crowd. I think she believes it makes her seem more down to earth. It doesn't. "We are so fucking going to rock this," she continues, talking just to hear herself speak. The rest of the band sticks to their vices and I'm pretty sure I see Kash and Dax buying acid from a trashy looking dude in a skirt.

I tug my ripped T-shirt down in the front and don't bother to fix it again when it rides up. I've worked hard to have a stomach worth showing off and I didn't get a tattoo below my belly button to keep it hidden. I trace my fingers over the angel wings and mouth the words that rest between them. *Real Ugly.* That's life. Fucking hideous and hateful and bloody. I wish I could see it otherwise.

"Don't let it get to you," America says from behind me. I jump a bit and almost knock over Terre Haute's front man, Rook Geary. He glares at me, but doesn't say a thing, sliding around me and disappearing into the darkness outside. The roadies rush the stage like fucking Oompa Loompas, dancing around and dragging equipment away, so they can set up for us. I almost feel sorry for them, but then I remember that half of them are here so they can fuck and buy drugs on a daily basis. Fuck them.

"Let what get to me?" I ask, but I already know what she's talking about. That damn video. That damn ass motherfucking video. I cannot even imagine who recorded it or how or why they've waited all this time to scare me with it. The events that took place on that screen happened when I was sixteen years old, and I just cannot figure out the time lapse. Unless, of course it was Hayden. Coulda been Hayden.

I watch her giggling and flirting with Dax, and I still find that pretty hard to believe. She might be a crafty bitch, but she's a crafty bitch without a brain. Still equally as threatening as whoever sent the video, but incapable of subterfuge.

"If you ever need to talk … "

"Yeah," I say as I take out another cigarette and find myself left with an empty pack. Fuck. I toss the box in the can and light up. "You're probably the last person I'd come to."

"Good," she says without even a hint of a smile. "Because I was going to tell you not to come to me. Talk to Blair."

"Hah. Thanks, America. Perfect fucking advice." I take a long, hot drag and let my head hang back, blonde hair teasing the bare skin of my shoulders. I can't imagine spilling my guts to anyone, let alone America. Even the thought of pouring my heart out makes me shiver.

I lift my head up and watch as our equipment is dragged out and positioned just so. Dax's drums in the back. Blair's keyboard on the right, just behind Wren's guitar. Kash's bass goes on the left side of the stage next to my Wolfgang. And Hayden, of course, goes right in the fucking center.

I close my eyes for a moment and tune out everything

— the crowd, Hayden, America. When I play, I dive so deep into myself that I come out the other side a different person. So introverted that I'm extroverted, you know what I mean? No. No, of course you don't. Nobody does, and that's always, always, always been my problem. I take a little note from Turner's book and throw some arrogance and swagger into my step before I move out, stepping over duct tape and cords, past the set list that's been stuck to the ground near my feet.

There's a crowd out there somewhere, a big ass fucking one, and in the back of my mind, I know that they're cheering for us, for me maybe, calling out the names of songs, pulsing and throbbing like a heartbeat. I sense them, but I don't see them; I don't hear them. My fingers slide under the guitar strap and lift it over my head. Settling that comforting weight over my shoulders makes me feel like I'm right where I was always meant to be. My hand slides up the neck and my fingers kiss the strings.

This fucking guitar costs more than any car I've ever owned, and I think I'm in love with it. Hell, I have more feelings for my Wolfgang than I've ever had for a living person. Call me cold if you want, but my guitar's never let me down. People have. You do the math on that one.

This baby lets me take my low E string from an E note to a D and back in a flash without having to retune. It

can cry like a baby and scream like a devil; it's got angel wings and horns both, and it'll kiss you at the same time it fucks you. Not many dudes can top that, right?

I close my eyes again as Hayden's voice switches gears in an instant – from wannabe rock star to freaking rock goddess. I don't know how she pulls it off, but when she's onstage, I forget to hate her so much. She's got lungs for days and a set of pipes that remind me of an old-timey organ mixed with the screech of eighties hair metal. I don't ask how that's even possible, but I do my best to enjoy it.

I let Hayden's voice in, but I refuse to accept anything else, continuing to block out the crowd while I find myself somewhere deep down and drag her screaming out the other side. By the time my fingers begin to move across the strings, I've got a smirk on my lips and a pair of dark sunglasses on my face. Don't know where those came from, but who cares? I could play in the dark; I could play blind. I don't need to fucking see to know that I'm rocking the crowd's collective face off.

I keep my gaze narrowed to a pinpoint in front of me, locking onto Wren as he swings his head down and smashes the stage with his feet, further riling up the sweaty, heaving mass in front of us. Hayden's already got them in a frenzy, sliding her fingers down her belly and teasing the edge of her pants. She knows how to put on a show; that's for sure. Lucky for us that most people think she's the hottest fucking piece of shit on two legs. In a genre dominated by cock, we've got the one thing that lets us breakthrough the walls of a stubborn crowd – a sexed up leading lady. I'm not proud of exploiting Hayden, but she seems okay with it, and I'm the first to take advantage.

"*Forget*," Hayden breathes, kissing the microphone, sucking it back with a heavy breath. "*Forget me forever. I've destroyed you one too many fucking times.*" Her chest rises and falls as she moans into the mic, drawing cheers and swirling up a mosh pit below the stage. Arms and legs fly out and flail about, lost in an ecstasy that transcends the physical and pulls the spirit out through your fucking nostrils, a modern day mummification through sound.

"*Bleeding, broken, buried beneath,*" I growl into the mic stand, doing my best to harmonize with Hayden and not overpower her. A part of me wishes I could, that I could take over the stage and stand under that spotlight, woo that crowd, bring them to their knees with my voice. The rest of me knows that'll never happen. I don't know if I've got the strength to spill my guts on stage like that. The guitar is hard e-fucking-nough; it teases the soul and nips at the spirit, but when I'm standing back here, I can at least pretend they don't see me open and bare before

them. Ignorance is bliss, right? *"Torn and trembling, take me in your arms, but know that it'll be the last time. The last. The last. The last FUCKING time!"* My scream echoes out and paralyzes the crowd, sliding through the gray matter between their ears, soaking in, tainting them with my poison.

Wren slides across the stage, and I move to meet him. We're just two dancers joining up for a waltz, spinning in circles with our music, stepping into one another and moving back. Our spines line up and we sink into that shit, fucking our guitars and grinding them into their crotches as we bleed pain and suffering and longing into the crowd. It's my music after all, so it's just reflecting what's inside. Hayden might sing it, but it belongs to me. Me. Me. Me.

Through my sunglasses, I see a face just offstage, hiding in the shadows with a smirk.

Turner. Turner fucking Campbell is watching me screw this crowd with my axe, and I can't breathe. For a moment, I'm afraid my fingers are going to slip, and I'm going to blow this whole gig, but the inner me, the one I dragged out, turns up the notch on my smirk and slides my tongue across my lips. *Oh my god! What the hell am I doing?* I flick it out and suck it back in, melding into Wren, sliding against him like we're screwing back to back. And I don't even like the guy. I don't like *either* of

these guys, but I can't stop myself. The music's taken over me, and will do what she fucking pleases.

I watch Turner watching me, and see that his brown eyes are glittering dark, like a night sky filled with stars. It's so off-kilter with his personality that it really throws me for a loop. Once again, I find myself having trouble hating him. Seem to be having a lot of trouble with my loathing abilities as of late. Guess when I get onstage, I am just fucked.

Our duet ends and Wren pulls away leaving me cold. And in the middle of an impromptu solo. Shit.

Luckily, Amatory Riot has functioned as a unit long enough for the others to follow me, modifying our song right then and there. The crowd goes fucking wild, and the air escapes my lungs. The lights overhead shift and I find myself bathed in color. My eyes shift to search for Turner again, and I'm glad I'm wearing these shades. If he knew I was looking for him, I'd never live it down.

A gasp goes up on my right and Turner appears out of nowhere, snatching my mic from its stand and grabbing Hayden around the waist. He makes a little *come on* gesture at me and then leans forward and grabs my lips with his.

I don't stop playing; I can't. Even if I wanted to, I couldn't stop the burst of fucking power that's just taken hold of me. I'm both a victim and a master to it as it

draws my hands along the neck and plucks strings with a violent fervor that both scares and amazes me. Hot wet heat takes over my mouth and pulls the rest of the inner me out, and then I'm kissing Turner back hard and fast and furious while the world's most intense riffs are just pulled straight through me, cutting me up and bleeding me over the stage.

When he pulls away, our eyes lock tight, and I know he can see right through my shades, through my head, and straight down into me. It's a trick; it's gotta be. I want to remember the way he spoke to me on the phone, the way he left that poor girl half-naked over the PA speaker, but I can't seem to grab any memories that haven't been made right here, on this stage. *What else is there?* my soul asks me as Turner uses the cord of the mic to spin it in a circle and snatch it back in one tattooed hand.

My solo comes to a natural end, and I fall right back where I left off, taking the band with me, opening my ears up to Turner's voice as it slides into the microphone. It's unbelievable – my words from his lips. I step back and Hayden moves up beside him, doing her best to out sex her colleague.

It doesn't work.

I don't think it's even possible to out sex Turner Campbell.

He grabs the hem of his shirt and slides it up, flashing his taut belly and a sea of tattoos against pale, sweaty flesh. His fingers rub the dark hair above his jeans and then drop the fabric back into place, much to the dismay of the crowd.

"*Tearing me up, shredding me inside; my walls are coming down in flames.*" Hayden's voice slides in alongside Turner's and for a split second there, I'm jealous. Of what and who and why, I have no idea, because I fucking hate them both, and they deserve each other, but … I brush the feeling aside and slam my axe to bits with my pick. "*If you break me, baby, be prepared to pick up the pieces.*"

Three. Two. One. And the song is over, and my pick is flying out across the crowd and landing in greedy hands. Sweat pours down my face in sheets and my body is wracked with violent trembles. Turner spins around and grins at me as the crowd explodes into a riotous fervor that makes the bouncers nervous. And they have every right to be. It is crazy hot up in here, and there's this primal vibe in the air that makes the hair on the back of my neck stand on end. I wet my dry lips and watch as Turner slides my mic back into place and snatches up a water bottle from the side of the stage. He takes a swig and then hands it over to me.

My hands drop down and take hold of it, even though

I'm not thirsty, even though I can't imagine anything as earthly as hydration. When he reaches out and plucks the shades from my face, I don't stop him.

"That was tight, Knox," he growls as he uses his middle finger to slide them up his nose. "Real fucking ugly."

CHAPTER 6
TURNER CAMPBELL

Show time.

I swipe my hand through my already sweaty hair and stalk onto the stage, listening with an inner smirk to the sound of the crowd going bat shit crazy for me. I pause behind the mic and slide one hand up the stand while I rest the other around the grip.

I wish Naomi were offstage watching me, but I already saw her make a run for it. As soon as Amatory Riot's set was done, she took off like a bat outta hell, bursting through the door backstage; she didn't even ask for her shades back. I wonder if she'll take me up on my offer for drinks tonight. She better after that little impromptu show we put together. Didn't expect that, but

it was fucking hot. My cock tingles at the thought and my tongue slides across my lips, boiling the crowd into a wild frenzy.

I thought Milo was going to wring my neck for that shit, but listening to him bitch was worth it. I can still taste Naomi on my mouth, hot and sweaty and perfect.

I have to have her.

My itch for info has become an all consuming burn, one that's eating me up from the inside out. I need to know who she is and where she comes from and then I have to make her mine for a little while. If I don't, I think I'll go fucking crazy. I've never felt this way before, and it's scaring the shit out of me. Mystery Girl's got me interested.

"Good evening, San Diego," I growl over the roaring voices below me. I feel like a fucking king up here, like I'm being worshipped. A smile crawls across my face. "Looking fucking beautiful tonight." I point to the prettiest girl I can find and tilt my head to the side. "I hope you liked my little prelude earlier." I pause and slide the mic slowly out of the stand. "But I'm fucking warning you because that was just a taste. I hope you've had a lot to drink because this is gonna hurt." I grin. "This is my hour to destroy you."

Treyjan starts up our most popular song, 'Breaking Pretty', and trashes the stage with his guitar. Jesse isn't

far behind him, cutting up the crowd while I bounce on my toes and swing my head in time to the music. The bass line sneaks in strong from Josh's side of the stage and punches the venue hard when Ronnie smashes his kit into the mix.

Instead of pushing Naomi out of my mind, I think about her hard. I imagine my body slamming into hers, imagine her back pressed up against a cold cement wall and her hot heat gripping me. I put that fire into my voice and snarl out the lyrics to the song, lacing them with sexual tension, with intensity, biting the words off and pissing all over that goddamn stage.

I don't care who graced it before me or who will stand here after; it's fucking mine.

"*You're body's soft enough to break and your pussy's hot enough to melt.*" I lift up my fingers and make an obscene ass fucking gesture that probably has Milo biting off his prissy, manicured little nails. "*That breaking pretty is leaving me blue, baby.*"

I spin in a circle and swing the mic around with me, tossing it up into the air, so I can catch it with my opposite hand. When my fingers wrap around it, the crowd starts to scream these blood curdling cries that make me hard as a rock and send chills down my spine.

"*And when you're gone, I'll still be left in pieces, scattered across the face of this motherfucking,*

godforsaken earth." The words are mine, right, because I fucking wrote 'em, but they're being stolen from me by Naomi friggin' Knox. I don't expect her to show up, but suddenly she's there and she's snarling onto Jesse's mic and eating up my lyrics.

Her blonde hair's stuck to her face and her lips are moist with sweat as she steps up beside me and tries to steal the friggin' show.

Fuck me.

I turn to face her, and I grin big, reaching out a hand for her waist. She pulls away and the people go nuts. A few even try to climb up the front of the stage in their frenzy and have to be picked up and hauled off by the bouncers in the black T-shirts. Nice to know they're useful for something.

"So put me back together, back to-fucking-gether, baby." Naomi's voice is crawling all over mine and she's marking the shit out of the stage, tearing it up and shredding it to pieces. White hot rage boils up inside of me and my harmonies blend into growls and then all out screams as we try to sing over one another.

My heart is thumping like crazy in my chest and feels like it's going to explode along with my cock. She turns and looks straight at me as her full lips mouth the words and beads of moisture drip down her bare belly. When she moves towards me, I reach out my arm again and

manage to sneak it around her waist, drawing our foreheads together, clashing our mics with a shrill shriek. Her hand finds my ass and draws the sunglasses out of my back pocket, hovering there way too fucking long to be played off as an accident. *She's feeling me up onstage. I think I'm in love with this girl. Holy shit. Who the hell is she?*

And then with our foreheads pressed together and our mouths nearly touching, I get this flash of memory that flickers like a bolt of lightning through my head and out the back of my skull. It's not there long enough that I can actually grasp it, but at least it's confirmation that I'm right. I know her. I do. I just don't know when or where or how.

Our bodies grind together, hips pressing close, denim against denim, and our free hands wander up and down, molten hot fingers pressing against bare skin, touching, hovering, absorbing. When Ronnie's solo rolls around, Naomi pulls the mic from my hands and slides my shirt up and off, tossing it to the wild-eyed monsters below.

They're circling and screaming, begging for blood, praying for us to fuck right then and there.

I see Milo at the edge of the stage, ready to move forward and put a stop to it all, and take my chance before it's too late, grabbing the mics back and literally tearing Naomi's shirt off her shoulders. Hell, it's ripped

anyway, so it comes off easy and ends up sailing into the hands of a dude in the mosh pit.

She looks so fucking fierce standing there in a red lace bra, tattoos winking at me from her chest and her belly in her too tight jeans and her fucking sick ass boots. I want her so bad it hurts, but when I move forward, she snatches the microphone from my hand and eats up the last words to my song, throwing the lyrics down so hard that I almost lose it. She's stealing the stage from me, taking it hard and riding it.

I do my best to take it back, but it's too late. The song ends. Naomi drops the mic to the floor and kicks it hard. I grab her wrist in one hand, but I don't know what to do with it, so I just watch as she slides her shades back on and smiles at me.

"Did you send it?" she whispers over the screaming fans, clamoring at the walls like soldiers in the midst of a fierce as fuck battle.

"Send what?" I growl at her, gripping too hard, squeezing too tight. I want to shake her and hug her and scream at her and fuck her, all at the same time. Goddamn it, my head is freaking killing me. What is with this chick and who the hell does she think she is? Why doesn't she worship me like everybody else? I'm so torn up inside that I feel like I'm going to split in half.

"Good," she says. "That's what I fucking thought."

And then she walks off stage and leaves me trembling with rage and lust both.

She never shows up for drinks.

CHAPTER 7
❧ NAOMI KNOX ❧

After every high comes a horrible fucking low.

I have mine on the bus the day after the San Diego show, lying on my side in the dark of my bunk with the curtain drawn and my iPod destroying my eardrums, playing Turner's music over and over and over again in my head. Somehow, I've got it in my mind that if I listen to it enough, the longing will go away.

It doesn't.

Instead, tears stream down my face, and I find myself obsessing over the date I'd promised I'd never obsess about.

March 15th.

Oh, how I hate March 15th.

It's three days away, and I can't stop thinking about it. Six years. It's been six years, and the pain is still as fresh as ever. *And it's all his fault. Him. Turner Campbell. Might as well change his name to Satan or Beelzebub or Lucifer or something.*

I touch a hand to my belly and roll away from the wall, so I'm facing the black curtain. My fingers play across the stitches while my mind tries to convince me to get up and take ownership over what happened on that stage. I should be proud; everyone else is. Except maybe Hayden. I mean, she says she's glad that we got some hot press, but I think she's jealous that I stole the spotlight from her. Hayden really, really doesn't like to share. I wonder, maybe, if it has something to do with Turner Campbell, too. If maybe she remembers she slept with him, and if she's jealous about the kiss.

Fuck.

How am I going to look him in the eyes again? If I do, he'll see things there that I don't want anyone to see. I'm not a sixteen year old girl with idol fantasies; I'm a grown ass woman, and I need to let up on this Turner obsession that I've been nursing. Shit. But I know deep down that I'm on his radar now. My mistake. I should've never returned his jacket to him. I'm such a fucking idiot.

I sit up suddenly and tear my headphones off, tossing them to the foot of the bunk and climbing out and into the

bright sunshine that's streaming through the windows. The door to the front is open, and I see the band sitting around and eating one of America's rare but admittedly delicious home cooked meals. Blows my fucking mind that the woman can whip up a five star dish on a bus. In-freaking-credible.

Everyone looks up as I walk in, and Spencer smiles at me in the rearview mirror. There's no doubt in my mind that they can see the tear streaks down my cheeks or the redness in my eyes. But fuck 'em. I don't care. Tears or no tears, I could still kick all their asses.

America assumes my expression has something to do with the video and gives me a sympathetic look. Good, but she has no idea how much worse this is. It's a scar that'll never heal, but one that I thought would at least scab over. *Thanks a lot, Turner. You're ripping it off, piece by piece.*

"I need to stop at a store," I say, and America's soft expression hardens.

"No problem, lemme just stop the caravan and tell all five bands and their staff to wait while you run in for some tampons." I flip her off and roll my eyes as I grab a plate and slap some food onto it. I'm not hungry and my stomach feels like it's full of lead, but I'm going to go through the motions, damn it.

"Fuck you," I tell her as I scoot in beside Hayden and

try not to touch her skin. You never know where it's been. "You know what I meant. When we get to Phoenix, I need cigs. Jesus Christ, who put a stick up your ass this morning?"

"You did," Hayden says, leaning her elbows on the table and resting her cheek against her hands. She stares at me with her blue eyes and smiles an evil smile that makes my already aching belly feel like it's being pulled in two directions. God, I might throw up. "Turner's been calling all night and all day." Hayden nods her chin at the counter, and I look up to see my phone resting there next to America's. Oops. Guess I forgot to drag it in my cave with me.

"So?"

"So, you know how I feel about him," America says as she switches off the stove and dumps whatever it is she's cooking onto a plate. "And I don't want Amatory Riot too closely associated with Indecency. It's only a matter of time before somebody dies or fucks up, and they'll be screwed. We don't need to be attached to a sinking ship." She punches the faucet on hard and starts to scrub, splattering her fancy suit with soap bubbles and droplets of dirty water.

"I had no idea you two were so into each other," Hayden continues, doing her damnedest to take my bad mood and bring it up to a whole new level. "Let's just

hope he's better in bed than I remember." Her smile remains stuck to her lips as she drags a bite of food up to her mouth and chews it slowly, like a fucking cow. My fingers clench around my fork, but I manage to resist the urge to stab her in the thigh with it.

"Interesting," I say, letting a smirk twitch on my lips. "That you remember fucking him at all. Glad you got your memory back though. Now you can owe me and Blair one for cleaning up your vomit and refraining from posting pictures of your puke covered ass online."

Hayden frowns, but before she can say anything else, Dax is sliding a box of cigarettes across the table at me.

"I know they're not your favorite, but it's better than nothing, right?" I clamp my hand over the carton and drag it back, feeling Hayden's eyes boring into my cheek. Good. Let her think that Dax and I have something going on. I think he's the only guy she's ever truly had feelings for. Hmm. Maybe I should start dating him just to fuck with her? I consider it for a moment. Anything that hurts Hayden makes me happy. Call me cold, but it's true. Misery loves company.

I light up and start smoking.

Dax watches me with gray eyes and then slides a cig of his own into his mouth. Soon, the whole table is lit up, even Hayden. Hey, you know what they say – the band that smokes together, stays together. It's a scientific fact

that cigarette smoking is a bonding exercise. Look it up.

"You really into that stupid fuck?" Wren asks, grinning at me and nibbling on the end of his cigarette like it's a stick of gum. A pair of black studs wink at me from between his brows, bouncing light across the ceiling. I doubt he even really cares about the answer to that question. More than likely, he's just trying to stir shit up. That's Wren for ya.

"I don't even know him," I admit, figuring the truth is better than any lie. "I slapped him in the face, so he's into me now. I think he just wants his balls back."

Wren and Kash laugh, but Dax narrows his eyes, like he can smell a secret hidden somewhere in my words. Turner could; I know that's why he spoke to me like that on the phone. He knows I've got secrets, and he'll do anything to pry them out. I've got to figure out a way to make myself a lot less interesting and fast. No more onstage stunts. Period.

I stab my cigarette out in an ashtray and stand up, dumping the rest of my food into the trash and tossing my plate onto the counter for America to clean up. One bonus of having a manager with OCD is that she'll clean shit up, if only to soothe her own anxieties. I snatch her tablet on the way out of my room and hold it up for confirmation. She nods at me and lets me disappear into the bathroom where I sit bare assed on the toilet and take

a piss. Flicking my fingers across the screen until I find the video of me covered head to toe in blood.

It's kind of hard to watch, but I make myself do it over and over and over again until my eyes hurt and the seat starts to dig into my butt. I'm trying to play Nancy fucking Drew here, searching for clues as to who could've filmed this. They would've been standing in the hallway with the camera or phone or whatever it was about waist high. This makes it even harder for me to make any deductions about height.

I stand up and fasten my pants with one hand while I continue to hold the tablet in the other.

Picture's a bit shaky, like whoever it was was scared – or excited. I mean, they didn't say anything, didn't try to stop me. The shot ends with me crumpled over the bed, sobbing. The scissors fall to the floor and stain it crimson. So ominous. So, so ominous, the sound of that blade falling. I don't think I'll ever forget it.

When I exit the bathroom, America shoves my phone in my face and snatches back the tablet.

"Deal with your shit," she tells me as I stare at the incoming call. Blocked number. Turner.

"What?" I snap as I answer it, crawling into my bunk, so I can at least pretend to have some privacy. A harsh chuckle slithers through the speaker and fucks my ear.

"Hey there," he says, like we're old friends. "Glad to

see that you're finally up and at 'em."

"Fuck you." I hang up and toss the phone down, knowing full well that when he calls me back, that I'll pick it up. Fifteen minutes pass. A half hour. Two.

When I fall asleep, I fall asleep dreaming of Turner soaked in blood.

Two secrets wrapped up in one and both ready to destroy me at the same time.

Great.

CHAPTER 8
TURNER CAMPBELL

I spend all day on the bus smoking weed and jacking off. I have to. Otherwise, my mind gets all wrapped up on Naomi fucking Knox. I'm so zoned into her right now that I didn't even take advantage of the girls waiting outside the door last night. They were all grayscale while Naomi was in full fucking technicolor.

Oh baby, you can bet your sweet ass I'm not giving up on you, I think as I stroke my cock to her image and lean my head back against the wall behind me. Any girl that can sour hot pussy for me is worth chasing. I bring up the memory of our foreheads pressed together and the sweat rolling down between her breasts and blow my load into my hand, tossing it into the sink and washing it

away before I get pissed again. Can't help it. My mood is night and day right now. One minute, I'm wanting to worship the ground she stands on, and the next, I want to destroy her.

She obviously doesn't like me, doesn't even respect me. But why? I comb my brain for that flickering punch of memory and can't find it.

"Fuck," I snarl as I kick open the bathroom door and stalk to the front of the bus. Nobody talks to me right now; they all know better. I rip the charger out of my phone and call Knox back. When she answers, her voice is groggy and far away, soft. My hard-on springs back with a vengeance, pitching a big ass tent right there for Josh to ogle. He rolls his eyes and turns away in the captain's chair, focusing his gaze out the front window.

"Hello?"

"You gonna stop hanging up on me, so we can talk?" She pauses, and I swear to Christ, I can hear gears in her head clicking as she realizes it's me on the phone. Man, she must be pretty tired if it took her this long to get that.

"What do we have to talk about?" she asks me, and I can hear blankets rustling. I wonder if she's masturbated to me yet. If she hasn't, she will. They always do. *Even if this one's different?* my mind asks me. I'm too distracted to pay it much attention.

"Well, you never showed up for drinks last night. I

was worried about you."

"Bullshit," she says, but her voice lacks any conviction, like she's too tired to even give me that emotion.

"And you owe me an explanation."

"Oh? Do I?" Naomi says sarcastically, and my fist clenches hard at my side.

"You asked me if I sent it. Sent what?"

"Go to hell, Turner." The phone crackles, and I think she's about to drop me again, so I speak quick. She needs to know that I know she has secrets. I could tell that from the moment I met her. It's a special trick of mine. I spent my whole life around people with dirty, little deeds to hide, so I consider myself an expert.

"Listen, babe," I say to her, wanting to make this pretty fucking clear. "I know we've met before. I may not remember when or where *yet*, but I will. You can bet on it." I pause and listen to her breathing for a moment. "And if it's one of those little secrets you want kept, come find me before I spill it."

This time, it's my turn to hang up on her.

I clench my hand around the phone and drop it from my ear, noticing as I start to turn around that Josh is glaring at me again. Maybe he doesn't like the way I talked to Naomi. So what? He doesn't know that I'm just fucking with her. I'd never tell, no matter what it was. I

may not have any secrets of my own, but I sure as shit know how to keep them. And let's be honest – most secrets are better left buried.

Phoenix is hot as fuck. No wonder I've never come here before. As soon as I step off the bus, sweat starts to pool on my lower back, and my head swims in the heat. It's the middle of the night for crying out loud, and the desert is still baking the shit out of this city.

I wipe my hand across my forehead and get out a cigarette, lighting it up before I start across the parking lot and catch a glimpse of Naomi moving across the pavement with a purpose in mind. She keeps looking over her shoulder like she expects something to leap out at her.

A grin spreads across my face.

I toss my cig down and hurry forward, cutting through the bushes and heading her off before she comes out the other side. When I step out at her, she doesn't scream, doesn't even flinch, just glares at me with her orange-brown eyes for a moment before taking out her shades

and slipping them on her face. It's dark out, so that means she's trying to hide from me.

My grin gets bigger.

"Hey there, in a hurry?"

Naomi ignores me and moves off into the darkness, blonde hair catching light from the street lamps and glowing as she moves between pools of brightness. *Angel, devil, angel, devil.* That's what she looks like as she crosses between light and dark. I follow a few steps behind her.

At the next intersection, she pauses and turns to look at me.

"Stalking is an actual crime, you know."

I shrug.

"Yeah, but walking to the gas station isn't. I can't help it if we're going to the same place." She continues to stare at me, and then turns away, letting smoke trail from her lips in a gray cloud and curl up and into her nostrils.

"What the hell do you want from me? You want to fuck me, is that it?"

I think about that for a minute and run my hand through my hair. That's a good question. What do I want with this girl? Even I don't know the answer to that.

"At first, I kind of wanted to punch you in the face," I admit. Turner Campbell doesn't keep secrets of his own, not even little ones. Learned my lesson by watching the

people around me fuck up royally, eaten alive from the inside. Stupid ass motherfuckers. Once it becomes a secret, it's hard to let it out. If you don't keep it inside to begin with, it doesn't get the chance to fester and rot. So, honesty is my policy. If it makes me a dick, so be it. "But now, yeah, I'd kinda like to fuck you."

"As long as you promise not to leave me half-naked with my panties down around my ankles," Naomi says with a sarcastic smile, and then starts across the street. I follow after her and flip off a trucker who honks at us when the light turns green.

"What the fuck are you talking about?" I ask her as I catch up and watch as she rolls her eyes at me. Naomi pauses at the island of cement in the center of the road and turns to face me with raised brows.

"Wow. You don't even remember that girl, do you?" she asks, sounding disgusted. I look her up and down, take in her white wife beater, her black jeans and the high heels she's got on. Fuck me. If I don't scratch this itch soon, I'm gonna have the bluest balls in the fucking country.

"That roadie chick? Yeah, I remember her. I'm not always shit faced, you know? I do have moments of clarity." I flick myself in the head and run my tongue over my lips, letting her take in the stud and pretend she isn't interested. From what I gathered onstage last night,

she wants me just as hard as I want her. She just doesn't know it yet. See, that's the fucking problem with keeping secrets. Once you've got a few, you get so addicted that you even start keeping them from yourself. Poor Knox. Good thing she's got me to liberate her. "Somebody walked in on us. Despite what you might've heard, I don't really like to have an audience."

Naomi's harsh laugh echoes through the darkness as she swipes off her shades and starts walking backward without even looking for traffic. It's a ballsy move, stupid, too. Fuck, I really do like this girl.

"You stupid, motherfucking, piece of shit asshole," she says as she sticks the sunglasses in her pocket and turns away from me, blonde hair whipping around in the hot, dry air. I take a deep breath and watch after her, feeling that anger boiling inside of me again. Something about her just pisses me off at the same time it gets me off. Jesus Christ.

"What?" I ask, throwing my hands up in the air. Naomi Knox is strange as fuck. I thought I was an expert on women, but this one is out of my range of knowledge. "What the fuck is it now?"

"That person that walked in on you," she begins, stopping on the sidewalk and turning back to face me with a crooked smile, one that's sinfully wicked. "That was me, and I wasn't impressed."

Aw, fuck me.

I start to move across the road after her and nearly get killed by a fucking semi carrying logs. Dirt and grit sting my eyes and push me back to the sidewalk as my heart frantically tries to explode from my chest. When I finally recover, Naomi's gone.

CHAPTER 9
❦ NAOMI KNOX ❦

I'll admit, seeing Turner almost get turned into hamburger meat really fucked with me. There was this second there where I really thought he was going to die, and I was mad at myself for not telling him. Yeah, the emotion was premature and stupid as shit, but now I know that at some point, I have to hunt the devil down and tell him what he put me through. I've been dragging this shit around for far too long, and it's getting old. If I'm ever going to escape really and truly, I've got to dig up my dirt and bury him in it, too.

I buy my cigs from the gas station and take them back to the bus where I search out Wren and score some coke off of him. It's not normally my drug of choice, but he's

got plenty to go around and I need something to keep me up. Sleeping equals dreaming and right now, I've got nightmares in spades. Besides, a cocaine high sounds real good right now. I can tweak all over my guitar, blow some minds with my music. I play really good when I'm high.

I lay out white lines on the table in the front and snort them in quick succession. Wren watches me from the doorway and crosses his arms over his chest. He looks pretty hot tonight, dressed in a black tank and a pair of tight as fuck jeans. He doesn't have any shoes on either, which is a kind of a thing for me. Only problem is I hate him. Too bad because I'm horny as hell right now. I try not to admit to myself that it's all because of Turner.

"You want to talk about something?" he asks me, but I sure as shit don't. Not yet. I want to get high first. I lean back and rest my head on the seat behind me, waiting for the drugs to take over and give me courage, euphoria, confidence. It'll do all that, you know? Yeah, it could kill me, and yes, it's stupid as hell, but I do it anyway. I'm not right in the head, never have been. That's a problem of mine, one that I intend to work on at some point. I wonder briefly if I'd had real parents, if things would've been different. If, instead of being shuffled from home to home, I could've lived in one place, how I might've turned out.

I open my eyes and sit up, brushing the thoughts away like cobwebs. Introspection never helps; it only gets me more tangled up in my shit.

"Want to make out?" I ask Wren, studying his strong face, his stubbly jaw and then watching as he pulls his lip down with his middle finger and flashes me the tattoo there. *Fuck Yeah,* it reads. I scoot over and wait for him to join me, putting a hand on his chest before we start anything. "I don't want to screw though," I tell him seriously. "Got it?" Wren just shrugs and wraps his arms around me, pressing his mouth to mine. I tangle my tongue with his and try not to imagine what Turner Campbell is doing right now, if he's dipping his dick into hot, wet heat and thinking of me.

Naomi, seriously? Why are you even going there?

I scoot onto Wren's lap and press the hard bulge in his pants against my crotch.

It's fun for awhile, until Hayden comes back, panting hard, face as white as a sheet. Wren and I both turn to glare at her.

"Naomi," she pants, cheeks as pink as the top she's got on. It's got friggin' Rainbow Dash on the front. Like, who the fuck over the age of ten wears a *My Little Pony* on their clothing?

"What?" I snarl at her as I shove Wren back and stand up. Whatever it was that I was looking for in him, I'm

not finding. I wonder if I should just fuck him, but I don't know if that'll help. If I'm honest with myself, I'm still carrying a big ass torch for Turner Campbell, one that I thought had gone out long ago. Guess it just got relit.

Apparently, Hayden doesn't like my tone and proceeds to rip into me.

"Hey, you stupid bitch, either come with me or not. If you don't, maybe I'll forget our little agreement and call the cops in Tulsa with an anonymous tip. Think the guy you stabbed last month will testify to your penchant for violence?"

I grab my jacket off the hook near the door and tear out of the bus on Hayden's heels, wishing I could just reach out and strangle her with her hair. She leads me around to the other side of the bus and down to the trailer that we tow behind it with our equipment inside.

I light a cigarette as we go, one that quickly gets forgotten when I see what Hayden wants to show me. The lit cherry tumbles through the dry darkness and hits the dirt at my feet.

On the side of the trailer, there's a message written in blood. Like a scene in a bad horror film, the headless body of a dead bird lies on the ground beside the wheel.

"Oh shit."

Thank God we don't have a show tonight.

After what I saw, my hands are shaking so bad, I can hardly bring the cup of water to my lips for a drink. Or maybe that's from the coke I snorted. Not sure which.

"Are you sure you don't want to call the cops?" Dax asks, hovering above me and Hayden like an overprotective brother. He likes to think he's one of the responsible ones in the group. Not true. The only truly responsible one of all of us is America.

"No, it's fine," she snaps at him as she paces back and forth, hands tucked into the pockets of her navy suit coat, bits of stray hair poking out of her slicked back bun. She looks frazzled which is pretty impressive. It's the first time I've ever seen her like that. "Spencer's probably already washed it off anyway." America pauses and looks down at Hayden and me.

The bloody words flip through my head on a continuous loop.

Hayden knows Naomi's truth. Keep your fucking mouths shut.

"You have no clue who might've done this?" she asks

in a very severe tone, one that brings tears to Hayden's blue eyes. *God, I can't stand that bitch. At least she isn't blaming me for this shit.* "Like, is there someone you might've told *something* to?" she asks, stressing the word for Hayden's benefit. Unfortunately, since Dax is standing there, she can't be anymore obvious, but I wish she could be. There's at least a fifty/fifty chance that Hayden isn't going to understand what America's trying to get at.

"Not a fucking soul," I say, and Hayden just shakes her head. Neither of us believes her, I don't think, but there isn't anything we can do about it, so I just walk away and try not to dwell on the idea that somebody just decapitated a bird (or judging from the amount of blood, probably three or four) and used its life force to write a threatening message. At least now I know I have a stalker of some sort.

Awesome.

I leave the bus, even as America shouts at me to get my ass back there and get ready to take care of something I should've taken care of a long time ago. The adrenaline from the message and the coke are melding together to make for one pretty amazing trip. I feel like a Titan as I storm through the camp and pause outside of Indecency's bus.

The bodyguard just stares at me like I'm an idiot.

"I'm here to see Turner Campbell," I tell him, which he's probably heard a thousand times before. The man, who's as big as an ox and twice as wide, folds his arms across his chest and sighs.

"He isn't here," he tells me and then shakes his head, continuing on before I get the chance to start an argument. I'm kinda glad because my fights never end well. Last month, I stabbed a rabid fan in the stomach with a fucking hunting knife. Thankfully, the charges were dropped, but I have to be more careful than that. Another incident could bring everything crashing down around my fucking head, and if I go to prison, I'm hanging myself with my sheets. I won't survive in there. "But he did tell me to expect you, so if you'd like to go up and wait, that'll be fine with me. I just have to pat you down for weapons first."

I stare at the man like he's fucking insane.

Expecting me?

Turner was *expecting* me?

That son of a bitch.

My blood goes hot and my heart cold.

"Thanks." I force the word out through tight lips and spin away on my heel, moving across the dirt in the direction of the gas station when a voice calls out behind me.

"Naomi?"

I turn around and find a blonde in dark washed jeans and a red T-shirt. I don't know his name, but I know he plays bass in Turner's band. He's standing on the bottom step of the bus and holding the screen open with one hand. In the other, he has a book. I trust him right away.

I take a step forward.

"Yeah?"

The man smiles.

"Hey, I know you don't know me, but my name is Joshua Drake. I was wondering if I could talk to you for just a sec? It's about Turner."

A smile stretches hard across my lips, and I head for the door of the bus with a very specific purpose in mind – pissing off Turner Campbell.

CHAPTER 10
❧ TURNER CAMPBELL ❧

I fuck around the city for awhile, hitting up a few bars and stumbling half-drunk back to the parking lot where the buses are parked for the night. I find a lot of girls that night, but I turn them all down. Cannot stop thinking about Naomi Knox.

That was her? I wonder for the hundredth time. I'm still having a hard time believing she was the one that walked in on me fucking that roadie. Was that when we first met? Is that why she hates me? Nah. Well, maybe a little. But that isn't it. There's something else, something more.

When I hit the bus, I pause next to our bodyguard – can't remember his name for shit – and squint at him with

tired eyes.

"Naomi stop by for me?" I ask, and the man smirks. Makes me want to hit him in the fucking face. Who the fuck does he think he is? "What's your problem, man?" I growl when he just stares at me. He doesn't speak, doesn't bother to answer my question, and I swear on my fucking cock that I'm about to fire his ass when I hear moans emanating out from the bus. Normally, I'd just ignore that shit, but the look on the bodyguard's face tells me that there's something else going on here.

I tear up the steps and pound down the bus into the bunk area, snatching Josh's curtain back so hard that it comes off the rod and falls to the floor.

Naomi Knox is completely topless, draped over Josh's shirtless chest with one of his gloved hands resting on her lower back. The blankets are covering their lower halves, so I have no idea how far this has gotten, but it doesn't matter; I'm seeing fucking red. I am blinded by it.

"What the fuck, man?" My voice explodes in a roar and next thing I know, I'm grabbing Josh by the hair and yanking him out of the bunk and onto the floor. Naomi rolls to the side and comes up on her feet behind me, dressed only in her fucking panties.

Josh comes up swinging and I'm glad to see that he's still got his boxers on. *Good. If he'd have fucked her, I'd have killed him.* Why that is exactly, I have no fucking

clue, but I'm drunk off my ass, and well, let's just say inhibitions ... what inhibitions?

"Screw you, you motherfucking whore," Josh screams as he smashes me hard in the jaw and sends me stumbling back into Naomi. "You don't deserve her. You don't deserve any woman, you piece of shit!" Soft flesh presses against me as Naomi and I collapse to the floor, and then it hits me, this memory of a girl pressed against into a bed, eyes wide with tears rolling down her cheeks. I can hear the words, *I love you,* over and over and over again, and then it just fades, blacked out by a rush of alcohol, and I'm up and swinging again.

Josh's nose cracks under my fists and blood sprays out across my face as I pummel him back against the bathroom door and pin him there nice and tight, getting so close up that we could fucking kiss.

"You touch her again, and I will fucking kill you," I tell him, watching his blue eyes shimmer with rage and his jaw shake. Josh is young, too fucking young, and he isn't one of us. I think that's what pisses me off so much. Jesse, Ronnie, Treyjan, and I went to high school together. We *survived* shit together. And then Travis dies, and we get this fucker as a replacement, this bottle sucking baby who can't even drink yet, and he ... he, what, Turner? What did he do wrong? I step back suddenly and throw my arms up.

Josh wipes his hand across his bloody face and glares at me, trembling like a fucking cougar ready to strike. He's not done yet, so I take another step back to get out of range.

Out of range of Josh that is; Naomi is a whole other story.

She spins me around and grabs my face in her hands, coming close enough that I can smell her – a mixture of cigarette smoke and laundry detergent.

"You are not a fucking hero!" she shouts at me, digging her nails into my cheeks and drawing blood. My hands come up and wrap her wrists tight, attempting to push her back, but she's stronger than she looks, and I'm drunk off my ass, so we end up in a complete standstill. "You're not saving me from anything!"

"Let go of me, you fucking cunt," I snarl as she presses her forehead into mine. I can hear Josh panting from behind me, and the rage boils up again. Now, I want to beat them both up, Naomi and Josh. I try to move her back with the weight of my body, but she holds tight and we end up crashing together, front to front, and then I find my hands sliding around her waist and caressing her body, feeling up the plump flesh of her ass, the gentle curve of her back, her tits.

She doesn't stop me, but she keeps yelling.

"You don't own me," she says. "You don't have any

claim on me, so what do you think you're doing? What is it that you want?"

"Right now, just you, baby," I tell her and then she's biting my lip and kissing me so hard that blood fills both our mouths as we crash our teeth together. She sucks on the piercing in my tongue and swirls her own around it, flicking the metal hard while she climbs me, wrapping her legs around me and relaxing the pressure on my face.

I slam Naomi's body back against the cabinets in the kitchen, and I forget all about Josh. I'm pretty sure he's screaming, too, but fuck him; she's mine now. Ah, and fuck, she tastes like dirty candy and blood and sweat and ash. Best damn shit I ever tasted. Period.

My hands move up her back and into her blonde hair, tangling and tugging and testing the limits, seeing how far she'll let me go before she stops kissing me and starts biting. I have a feeling that in this case, the bite really is worse than the bark.

Naomi's nails gouge my back, digging into my flesh through the shirt before she finally takes it in two strong fists and rips it up and over my head, breaking our kiss for a moment and somehow cranking up the heat in the bus by a notch. That little burn I've got going for her turns into raging flames as I drop my head and brush a kiss across the tattoo on her chest. I'm too drunk to really register what it means right now, but I'm pretty sure it's a

broken, bleeding heart.

I nibble on Naomi's nipple, sucking the hard pink flesh into my mouth and rolling it around, making sure the stud on my tongue teases it mercilessly. My eyes flicker up and find Naomi's. They're starting down at me, wide and pissed. She's angry. Good. I like angry sex, and fuck, I'm angry, too.

I grin at her, and she grabs my chin, pressing her mouth to mine as I reach down and undo my pants, pushing them down my hips as far as possible without having to separate my lips from Naomi's. My cock springs free and my fingers push aside her panties, teasing the hot wetness there as I get ready to thrust in, to finally scratch that itch.

"God, you're gonna love this, baby," I snarl as she nibbles my lip, and then like a fucking tiger, she's swiping at me and cracking her palm against my face, nails slicing me good and spilling hot blood down my cheek. To say that I'm shocked is a friggin' understatement. Talk about mixed messages. What. The. Fuck.

I throw Naomi off of me and step back, stumbling over my fucking jeans and ending up looking like a fucking tool on the floor of the bus. She stares down at me, and her lip twitches in disgust. The expression's a far cry from the one she had just a moment ago.

"Not again," she whispers. "Never again."

And then she spins away and disappears naked into the night.

CHAPTER 11
NAOMI KNOX

I thought I'd feel good fucking with Turner. Instead, I just feel sick and weak and end up collapsing into bed, coke be damned. When I dream that night, my head is full of blood and birds and gravestones. Not exactly the best images to wake up to.

The morning doesn't get any better; Hayden is whining about not feeling safe, and America is talking about hiring us a bodyguard while Dax postures around the bus with his eyes narrowed out the windows, looking for some mystery culprit that he's supposedly going to destroy when he finds them.

I sigh and ignore them all, climbing into the shower and turning on the water as hot as I can get it.

I don't want to talk about the bird thing anymore – it's just fucking weird. Demented. Insane. It has to be the person who sent the video, obviously, but that doesn't help me figure out a possible culprit. In fact, it makes it even harder for me to hazard a guess. I just want to ignore it and hope it goes away. I can only handle one detrimental, life altering secret at a time surfacing, and it seems like I'm about to drown in the Turner thing.

Why is this so freaking hard for you, Naomi? Just walk up to the man and say, 'Hey, you helped me out once, but then you ruined me. I loved you, and you broke me.' I shiver. Yeah, I'm sure that would go over real, real well. I wash myself quickly and get out, stepping out of the bathroom in just a towel, and find myself face to face with Turner.

His hands slam against the wall on either side of me and force me back a step, effectively pinning me in the tiny square of tiled spaced in front of the toilet.

He's glaring at me, and his dark eyes are fierce, cutting through the air between us like swords, slicing up the silence and shedding its blood. His lips are pursed so tight that the piercings on either side are poking out at me like accusatory fingers. He's got on a black Amatory Riot shirt, and this time, I know he knows exactly who we are.

"*Turning the Key on the Past?*" he asks me, stating the name of one of our most popular songs. "Is that

supposed to be subtle, Knox?" My lip curls up in the corner, and I wonder where the fuck the rest of my band is, where America and Spencer are, and why they just let him walk in here like this.

"I don't like people in my face, Turner, so back the fuck off. And don't call me Knox. This isn't the fucking military. The name's Naomi." Turner slams his palm against the wall hard.

"Who are you?" he screams at me, and I have to resist the urge to knee him in the nuts. I'm pretty fucking sure that the asshole would press charges, and with last month's fiasco combined with the bird murderer psychopath fuck, it's just too risky. "And what do you want from me?"

"Want from you?" I ask with a bitter laugh. The towel slips and I just let it go, standing there proud and pissed and naked and fierce with hot moisture clinging to my skin and wet hair kissing my lips. Turner's eyes fuck me from head to toe and the leg of his pants bulges with the swelling of his cock. "Sort of seems like you're the one that wants something from me. You've been pursuing me, remember? You're the one that's following me around like a lost, little, puppy."

"Fuck you," he spits, stepping closer to me, driving me back. His skin is covered in sweat and his hair is mussy. I'm doubting he got any fucking sleep last night.

Good. He can suffer along with me. "You seem to know me a hell of a lot better than I know you. I want to know why. You a stalker or something?"

I spit in his face and he reaches out suddenly and snatches my wrist, dragging me forward and pressing me against the length of his body. His cock grinds into my crotch and his lips graze mine. But I'm not afraid. I'm not afraid of anyone or anything. My hand travels up the wall in the bathroom and slips into the tiny drawer on my left. The hunting knife appears in my hand.

"You want the short answer or the long?"

"Don't you think you owe me both?" Turner asks, and then I've got the blade up and forward, pressing into his throat, teasing blood, loosing his grip, pushing him back into the row of bunks. I don't look at the star tattoos near his hair or the sleeve of color that crawls up his muscular arm; I just look into the black devil heart of a man who doesn't care, who can't bother to care, who's too entitled to see what's right in front of him.

"From the trailer park, a rising star," I say as I quote a magazine article I read so long ago. I think I was sixteen then and Turner was twenty-one, the perfect idol. "I thought you were so amazing." I laugh, harsh and dry. "God, I should've known better." I drop the knife and step back. Turner lets me go, watching me with wide, wide eyes. "I worshipped you back then, you know? I

thought that if you could do it, if you could escape the hell you grew up in and make something of yourself, so could I. And the idea that you could use music to do it? Well, shit, Turner, I thought I was in love with you."

"You're the girl … the one … "

Turner stops talking and runs a hand through his blue-black hair. I let the knife fall to my side and look down at his hand, at the wolf tattoos and the paw prints etched into his skin. The only sound on the bus is the soft drip, drip, drip of water on the floor as it slides over my suddenly hot skin and is replaced almost immediately with sweat. Angry tears prick my eyes.

"I went to your show in Tulsa when I was in a bad place. Made the mistake of hitching a ride home with an older guy." The memory runs through my mind and rage explodes in my skull. "He told me I owed him for the ride home, and pushed me over the trunk of his car. He was going to rape me, but you helped me stop him, do you remember that?"

"Naomi Knox. Oh my fucking God." Turner grips his head hard, and his eyes go wide. He's not looking at me anymore, but at my ankle. Where the tattoo is. The one that says *Turner Dakota Campbell*. Suddenly, he's exploding into action and scrambling at his shirt, tearing it away from his skin and throwing it to the floor, scratching at his back like he's got an itch. When he turns

around, I see it. It's still there, surrounded by paw prints in the center of his shoulder blades. *Naomi Isabelle Knox.*

Turner spins back around and just stares at me with wide eyes and a heaving chest.

"You slept with me and then you left me, Turner." The knife falls to the floor with that same sound, that very same sound, crowding my head with memories, lacing my chest with pain. "You left me there, and then I got pregnant, and I had to make the hardest choice I've ever made. I had to say goodbye to your baby, Turner, and then I had to start over again."

I take a step backwards into the bathroom and slam the door in his face.

CHAPTER 12
TURNER CAMPBELL

I kind of wish for a moment that I really had been hit by that semi last night. It would've saved me the trouble of getting completely and utterly fucking flattened by Naomi's words. If I said I felt like a bit of roadkill that'd just been scraped off the highway, I'd be telling it to you lightly. I mean, fuck. Fuck. Fuck.

What kind of tool has no idea what name it is he's got tatted on his friggin' back?

"Jesus Christ." My hands are shaking, and my brain is scrambling to pick up the pieces of that night. I was so fucked up that I can't even remember what it was that I was fucked up *on*. As for the tattoo … I've got so freaking many – half of them when I was out of my

friggin' mind. Shit. Shit. Shit. "Naomi!" I start to pound on the door, but she won't answer me. I don't even hear crying or anything, just dead fucking silence. "We've got a kid?" I keep pounding, hitting my fists against the flimsy wood, hoping it'll just shatter to pieces for me. *How could that have happened? I never forget condoms. Never.* "Fucking hell, Knox, open up!"

All the yelling drags that pretty boy drummer fuck back onto the bus and straight towards me. I back up before he can touch me and throw my arms into the air.

"I'm not looking to start shit," I tell him, as he glares at me for a moment and then glances down and sees the knife. His eyes flicker up and the muscles in his face tighten. Shit. This is a far cry from the way he looked at me the other day, like I was untouchable. Maybe Naomi's lack of respect for me is wearing off. I ready myself for a fight and pause only when the bathroom door slides open and Knox steps out dressed in a wife beater with no bra, tiny ass shorts, and knee high boots. Her hair is loose and wet and between her lips is a lit cigarette. A pair of sunglasses covers her eyes and shields her expression from me.

"Naomi," I say, and it kind of freaks me out the way my voice sounds. It's soft. Too soft. I steel my shoulders and try to get angry again. "You can't just tell me half a truth and leave it at that. I want to know everything." I

look at Dax, at his perfect emo bitch cut and the way he's looking at me like I'm the scum of the earth, and for a second there, I almost believe it. I figure she doesn't want her secret spilled, so I try to redeem myself a bit by holding back on the details.

"God, stop being such a whiny, little bitch, Turner, and get over yourself." Naomi moves forward and Dax lets her pass. Me, not so much. When I move to circle around him, he puts out an arm and forces me back, leaning close enough that I can smell the mint gum on his breath. I meet his heated gaze with one of my own and try to keep my temper in check. If I start a fight right here, things could get bad for me real fast. I can't deal with the cops today.

"Leave her the fuck alone, Turner. I'm warning you." And then he steps back and adjusts the skeleton gloves on his fists, watching me with narrowed eyes as I scoot past and chase after Naomi. That motherfucker doesn't scare me. Nobody does. Nobody can. I've been through enough in my life. I had a meth addict for a mom and several different step-daddies who graced the stained couch in our trailer. This is small potatoes compared to that crap.

"Naomi, wait up." I follow after her, realizing only after I've left the bus that I'm still shirtless. The sun beats down on my skin and sears me with hot, white heat.

Desert heat. It's a special flavor all its own, you know? I wrap one arm across my chest and squeeze my bicep with tight fingers.

She doesn't stop walking, but she doesn't try to outrun me either. She just keeps moving across the parking lot like she's got a purpose in mind and doesn't care if I come or not. Fine. I can deal with that. What I can't deal with is finding out I have a freaking kid.

Shivers travel up and down my spine, and it's got nothing to do with the damn weather.

"Boy or girl?" I ask quietly when I'm standing shoulder to shoulder with Naomi. Her face is still, and she seems okay, but the aura around that chick is toxic. If I had special powers or something, I bet I could see a black cloud billowing around her body. I stand close enough to burn.

"Trying to figure out what to have for dinner tonight?" she jokes, making a lewd gesture with her fingers and tongue. "I had no idea you swung both ways. Must be nice though, right? More bodies to choose from." My lip curls, and I have to really resist the urge to grab her by the shoulders and shake her. I don't know why I'm suddenly feeling like she's fragile all of a sudden. This is the same chick that slapped me in the face, but yet … she just can't be. She worshipped me? I can't imagine this girl worshipping anyone, but then again, she's got a big

ass tat of my name on her ankle. I wipe a hand across my sweaty brow.

"Our kid," I state, wondering where he or she is and how I'm gonna find them. Because I am. Hey, it might sound corny, but growing up without a father makes me determined as shit to be one. A good one. I take this crap seriously. "Girl or boy?" Naomi continues to smoke her cigarette and says nothing, heading in the direction opposite the gas station we visited last night.

"Does it matter?" she asks, and I can't help it. I step in front of her and stop her in her tracks, reaching out to grab the shades before she stops me with a hand to the wrist. Her silver fingernails wrap my skin and squeeze tight, sending a rush of hormones through me that I don't completely understand. This girl has strapped me onto a fucking roller coaster. I'm up; I'm down. It's giving me a fucking stomachache. "Those assault charges you threatened before go both ways, Turner, and I'm not trying to sound sexist, but it's a lot easier for a woman to level them against a man than vice versa, you catch my drift? It's just the way this horrible, ugly world works." Naomi releases me and steps back, pulling the sunglasses off herself. Her eyes are like nothing I've ever seen, a color that there's no name for yet. They match the desert, red and orange and brown, dry, seemingly barren. Behind them though, behind them there's a whole world

hidden beneath the dirt, one that can spring to life with just a drip of rain.

I wipe my hand across my face to help clear my mind. What am I now? A fucking poet? Naomi is just a girl I had drunk sex with a long, long time ago. She isn't an enigma or a mystery, just the one person I made such a stupid mistake with. That's all there is to it.

"Where's my kid, Naomi?" The edges of her lips droop for a moment before something clicks and she lifts her chin defiantly. The wind teases her hair and draws her nipples to hard points under the thin fabric of her shirt. If I were to reach out a hand and touch them ... I bite my lip so hard it bleeds and keep my eyes focused on her face.

Behind us, the camp is starting to come alive in anticipation of the show tonight. I have a hard time even imagining getting through it. I don't handle life altering revelations very well. They've never been very good to me in the past. *Fuck, this is exactly why I hate secrets. Just when you think everything is peachy fucking keen, some shit has to get stirred up to ruin the day.*

I run my tongue across my lips to wet them; this damn desert air is drying me out.

"Please," I say. It takes a lot of effort to get that word to pass between my lips. *Please* sounds like begging and Turner Campbell does not beg. Naomi's eyes flicker

away and focus on some shrubs at the edge of the parking lot. There's a lot more to this story than first meets the eye, that is for fucking sure. There are secrets wrapped in secrets buried under secrets; I can smell 'em from here. "Come on, Knox, you owe me an explanation."

Her eyes snap back to mine and her full mouth tightens into a thin line.

"Turner," she says, stepping forward and poking me in the chest with the corner of her sunglasses. "I don't owe you shit. Fuck off and leave me alone. Stop calling me, stop following me, and you better keep your ass off the stage when I'm on it. Me and you, we have nothing to say to each other."

And then she steps around me and leaves me in the dust.

CHAPTER 13
❧ NAOMI KNOX ❧

I survive the show that night – barely. I play, but I don't play with any heat or substance, and I can tell the crowd knows it. I mean, they still cheer and scream and flail, but they don't drop their inhibitions; they don't evolve backwards and fall to the floor in howling fits of animalistic rage. When they do that, you know you've nailed it. That night, I do good, but I don't blow anybody's mind.

Can't say the same for Turner.

From what Hayden says, he destroyed the stage and caught that whole damn building on fire with his words. She says they were so laced with rage that he was spitting acid and burning holes in the fucking stratosphere.

Good for him.

After our set, I retreat back to the bus and fall asleep.

When I wake the next morning, I can't hold it back. I end up at the table in the front with my notebook open flat and my pen pressed so hard against the pages that the paper tears with every other word.

Blair and Dax watch me silently from across the table while the rest of the band put-puts around the bus like they've got nothing better to do. And I mean, hell, fuck 'em, I guess they don't. They know when I'm like this that something good's coming. Our last album? Yep. Happened just like this.

"You want to take a break?" Blair asks after a little while, scooping some of her bi-colored hair over her shoulder and adjusting the little black and white polka dot bow she's stuck in the front of it. She looks cute, very vintage. Me, on the other hand, I look like shit. I haven't showered or changed my clothes, and I know I probably smell like sweat and beer, but when I'm writing, nothing else matters.

I shake my head and wish I could confide in her. It might make me feel better if I shared my secrets with somebody I actually like. In fact, I think given the opportunity that Blair and I could be best friends. And I don't mean that in the whole shallow sort of, *We like go every Friday and get our nails done together* bullshit. I

think Blair and I could be bury-the-body best friends. Too bad the walls I've put up are taller and longer than the Great Wall of China.

"Can I make you some coffee or something?" Dax asks next, uncrossing his long legs and standing up to stretch. "Something black, bitter, and cheap?"

I groan low in my throat and lean back, letting my head fall to the cushion behind me.

"Sounds amazing. Make a big pot and don't expect to share." I hear him laugh, but don't look up. Instead, I close my eyes and start to hum, putting my words to music. In a minute here, I'm gonna get up, grab my guitar and some headphones and fumble my way through to something epic. Works every time. It's just the way I roll.

"You gonna let us read any of that?" Blair asks as I sit up and open my eyes, glancing down at the mess of words that'll eventually turn into a song of some sort. Hopefully a good one. I shrug and spin the notebook around. All of my secrets are sitting there in code, hidden between the blue lines with cryptic phrasing and a horrible abuse of the English language that makes it nearly impossible to guess what I'm hinting at. There's enough to give people pause, to open up the idea of discussion, but nothing too personal, nothing too incriminating. And that's just the way I like it.

Blair reads the words carefully and taps her fingers on the table to get some kind of a rhythm going, and Dax steps up behind her, smelling like canned coffee and weed. The smell is oddly comforting, enough so that I shake out my hands and take my first breath in almost twenty-four hours. It hurts so much that it feels good, you know what I mean? It breaks up the tension in my chest and puts the briefest of pauses on my anxiety about tomorrow. March 15th. The six year anniversary of … *that*.

I made the right decision then, and I still stand by it now, but that doesn't mean I can't feel hurt about it, betrayed even. I trusted Turner, looked up to him then, and he took advantage of me and left me with a problem I wasn't ready to deal with yet. Fucking asshole. I pull out a cigarette and light up, taking small, useless puffs and blowing the smoke out in rings. Yeah, I can really do that.

"Lemme guess," Dax begins, watching me from under a dark mop of hair that falls across one of his gray eyes. "You can tie a cherry stem into a knot, too?" I grin and blow out another ring, watching as his eyes fall to the page and move down the row of illegible phrases I've just scribbled. I don't answer his question, but in case you're wondering, that would be a big, fat yes.

I lean back again and cross my arms over my chest,

trying to push Turner's face out of my mind. I want to tell him everything, or I did rather, but then he had to go and throw out that *you owe me* bull which just makes me want to hit him. And he kept saying *our kid, our kid.* There is no kid, and there's definitely no *our,* just a ghost of a memory that haunts me every damn day. Turner Campbell may not be the sole reason that I have trust issues, but he sure as shit didn't help. He could've cured me, I think, but instead, he dragged me backwards and left me in this state. Angry. Distrusting. Determined.

I finish my cigarette and flick it in the ashtray near my elbow.

"Jam with me?" I ask them, and get two surprised faces in response. Normally, I write songs on my own, and when I'm happy with what I've got, I show my shit to the band and let them layer in their own parts (so long as they don't fuck with my riffs). Today, I'm feeling social. Could be the death of me.

Blair and Dax exchange a look.

"Oh, come the fuck on," I say, slapping my palms flat on the table and standing up. "I didn't ask you to join me in holy matrimony; let's just play some shit together." I move away from the table and pause when my phone starts to buzz on the counter, shaking like an epileptic in a fit. I pick it up, glance at the number and then move over to the sink.

"Turner?" Blair guesses, and I nod as I turn on the water and drop the phone into the drain on the left – the one with the garbage disposal. A second later, I flick the switch and a horrible grinding, screeching sound emanates from down below. It's like an alley cat got in a fight with a semi-truck – and won.

The noise is enough to bring America sprinting from the back, iPhone still pressed to one ear, perfectly polished and shimmering in a nude suit and black pumps. She looks like she's on her way to a luncheon at the country club, not a rock concert.

"What in the God's name of fuck was that?" she snarls, and I smile, happy to see that our language is really rubbing off on her. I turn off the disposal and the water and step back, spinning to face her with a nasty grin.

"Just taking out the trash is all."

The jam session with Blair and Dax goes so fucking well that I almost forget about Turner and the half-secret I shared with him. The one that I'm going to have to finish sometime in the near future. After all, if I learned one

thing from trying out my new song, it was that it wasn't finished. The story that it's based on doesn't have an ending, so how can I expect the tune that's based off it to?

Anyway, I'm smoking a cigarette and watching the roadies unload our shit when he saunters up behind me and blows smoke in my ear. I'm so not worried about running into him that I don't even bother to turn around. I've got my music high right now and there is nothing in this fucking world that can beat that. Even crackhead Wren agrees with that one.

"Why are we playing Tucson when we skipped LA? Seems kind of fucked up, huh?"

I don't answer the question because I'm actually kind of shocked to hear his voice. For a few blissful, perfect hours there, he did not even fucking exist. I don't answer the question and instead keep my gaze focused on Spencer's back. She has these bright, butterfly wings tattooed on her shoulder blades, the perfect compliment to the creamy mocha color of her skin. I admit, I'm kinda jealous. My skin is so pale that all my tats look like stickers, like they've just been stamped there and aren't really a part of me. Pisses me the fuck off.

"I think I was pretty clear when I told you to stay the hell away from me, Turner." I drop my cigarette to the ground and watch as he steps up next to me and puts it out. My gaze remains focused straight ahead. I start to

hum the melody to the second new song I started today, the one about dead birds. Yep, even stalkers can be inspirational. My mind wanders back to *that* issue for a moment and quickly dismisses it. One thing at a time. That's about all I can handle right now.

"Yeah, but, uh, Knox, finding out that you and I procreated ties us together just a bit more than your typical set of strangers, huh?"

I shiver and pull out another cigarette. The lights of the venue are casting strange shadows around us, making the air look like it's full of ghosts. I wonder briefly if one of them is our kid and then shake off the guilt with a violent snap of my head, giving Turner my best narrow-eyed death glare.

"Really? You're going to pull that bull now? Why? Because you have daddy issues and need to soothe your tortured soul? Give me a break, Turner, and get the fuck over yourself." He's staring straight back at me, and his face is changing from soft and understanding to pissed off. Apparently, I said something I shouldn't have. Oh well. What's new?

"You don't know shit about me," he growls, clenching his fists so hard at his sides that his tattoos look like they're about to pop off and take flight, join the ghost-shadows flitting in the air. "So stop feeling sorry for yourself. I didn't purposefully try to fuck with your life.

We screwed, and I left. It wasn't you; it's just what I do. Girls proposition me; I fuck them. It's life. It's nature, whatever. We had a good time, and you got pregnant. It happens." Turner pauses, and I think I hear him mumble something like, *just not to me.* His callous attitude about the whole thing makes me want to rip off his balls, but then I remind myself that I'm not supposed to care. Slicing off some of his prized man bits would show too much emotion, so I grab the rage that's boiling inside, and I put a lid on it, clamp it down and keep it hidden. Later, tonight, when I get a hold of my guitar, I'm going to take a note from this dickhole and play it so hard it bleeds.

"Glad to know that that night meant so much to you." I smile and start to walk away. Being around Turner is not a good idea. I knew that when I was offered this gig; I should've walked away then. Now the noose he threw around my neck so long ago is starting to choke me. And I thought I'd chucked it? Pathetic. Even now, even as I'm standing here hating him with every ounce of my being, something about him is drawing me forward. Could be the fire in his brown eyes, the color that burns there so bright it blinds. Despite his callous attitude and his *all be damned* bullshit, Turner has enough passion to light the sky on fire. He does it with his music, but for some reason, it doesn't seem like he's capable of translating the good in him to real life.

I can't be around someone like this.

I have a hard enough time with my own issues. I need to be around people who know what they want and how to take it, who understand their strengths and play them hard, who fight to overcome their weaknesses. That is, if there are any people like that who actually exist.

Turner paces alongside me, all tight, twitching muscles and clenched teeth. He brushes the hair off his sweaty forehead with an angry hand, and I know he wishes he could just hit me. Glad to see he isn't sexist, that he'll attack any threat head on. But if he touches me, he's going down. I am a lot stronger than I look. I've been fighting off men twice my size since I turned ten.

"You know what I meant," he grounds out, tucking his hands into the pockets of his too-tight jeans. They kiss his skin so tight that I can practically hear the smacking of lips. That denim is freaking *painted* on Turner's legs. Doubt there's room for underwear in there.

"Do I?" I ask him, forcing my steps to slow, so he has a chance to explain himself. Right now, I'm heading straight toward Dax and Kash. Once I get there, Dax will chase Turner off. Or he'll try anyway, and I really, really don't want to deal with that shit. *So hurry up then,* my logical mind tells me. I ignore it, much to my detriment, I'm sure.

"I just meant that it wasn't personal, Naomi. I didn't

mean for this to happen to you, and I … " Turner trails off, and I have no choice but to turn and look at him. The sound of his voice was … strange, like he was embarrassed about something. I can't even imagine the man having that emotion, so it's a pretty big deal to me.

I stop walking, and Turner does the same.

"What?"

He looks at me like I'm crazy and steps back, running his fingers through his blue-black hair. The star tattoos on the edges of his hairline flash at me, highlighted by the bright lights on the sign at my back, the one that has both our bands' names plastered across it in two foot tall letters.

"I've never forgotten to use a condom before. Not with anyone. Not even once." I laugh so hard that tears come to my eyes, and I have to bend over to take a breath. Blonde hair falls over my shoulder like a curtain and obscures my face.

"Really? Is that the best line you've got, Turner? Jesus, I thought you were better than that."

"It's true," he snaps, voice so rough that I have to look up at him. His eyes are narrowed on me, and his full lips are flat and straight. He looks like a different person when he's pissed. The Turner Campbell I'm used to seeing is always smirking and is so cocky and arrogant, that anger doesn't even seem to be an option. After all, to

be angry about something, it has to bother you, and Turner likes to give off this impression that he's immune to the world. Or above it. Probably both.

"And I'm supposed to believe that shit?" I say as I stand up and reach my hands into my bra, adjusting the girls for maximum cleavage exposure. Turner watches with hungry eyes, and starts pitchin' a tent, if you catch my drift. Glad to see that I'm not the only one with a sweaty back and a pulsing crotch. *So we have sexual chemistry, how is that surprising? You're both young, relatively good looking, it happens. Just remember what happened last time you gave into it.*

I take a step back.

"If you can't even remember us fucking, how do you know that's true? How many girls have you fucked that have escaped your recent memory, hmm? There could be a dozen Campbell bastards running around by now."

"No."

That one word is strong as steel.

Turner and I stand there staring at one another with this sort of burn in the air between us, like we're both about to catch on fire.

"I know what happens to kids who grow up without dads."

"They turn into rock stars?" I say, and immediately regret it. I don't know why. The guy plucked my cherry

from the tree, ate it, and ran off before I woke up after. He didn't use a condom (maybe half my fault, but shit, I was the inexperienced one in the situation) and left me pregnant, homeless, and confused. The idol I'd looked up to had been relegated to devil, and I had a person growing inside of me who needed things, things that I couldn't give or didn't know how to give. Food, shelter, clothing. Love. Most especially that. And stability. You can't give something you've never had. Check the laws of science; it's impossible.

"I know that you're the only one. Don't ask how, but I just know." Turner shrugs and then sighs, dropping his anger into the hot desert air before reaching for a joint he's got hidden in his front right pocket. He offers it to me, but I decline, and he lights up. "I also know that you hate me, and that you're pissed at me, and I get it. Believe it or not, but I do." Turner puffs on his joint for a moment. I watch him and wonder why my knees are starting to feel weak and why my thighs are shaking like they can't hold the weight of my life anymore. I hate that feeling. Makes me sick to my stomach. I wait for it to pass. "But I want my kid, Naomi. No matter how you feel about me, how little you think I deserve him or her, I have a right to know everything. Bringing a person into this fucked up, shitty existence is something I don't take lightly. Wherever they are, I'll find them."

My throat is dry now, and I'm having trouble breathing. I swear to god that I'm about to pass out. I want to blame it on the heat, but I can't. It's Turner. It's always been Turner.

"What if you had to quit?" I ask him, voice breathy. Turner hears it, too, and takes a step forward, wetting his lips, holding his hands out, so that his fingers brush the thin hairs on my arms. I hate him, and yet I want him so bad it hurts inside. But after what he did to me, can I ever forgive him? Do I want to? Why am I even asking myself these stupid fucking questions? Even if I did admit to myself that in some fucked up, Stockholm syndrome type of way that I liked him still, he'll never change. He's always be an arrogant, cocky whore, and there's nothing I can do about that. "What if you had to quit the fucking and the drugs and the booze and the … " My words trail off and my breath catches in my throat as Turner leans in so close that I can see the beads of sweat on his upper lip, hear the thumping of his heart. "And the music? Would you do it?"

"Well," he begins, and I realize now that I'm paralyzed, that I can't drag my eyes from his. I should be kneeing him in the balls right now, watching him suffer with glee, but instead I'm standing here and breathing in the smoke from his joint, gazing at him like one of his stupid groupies. Fuck me sideways. "I know that I love

that kid. I know for sure, even without meeting 'em. I mean, with you as a mother and me as a father, how could we go wrong?" Turner tries to grin, but it falls flat. He's trying to come across as self-assured, but it isn't working. He's nervous right now, and he's thinking too much and too hard. My guess is that he's been thinking about this non-stop since I told him. "And I'd do anything for love."

I swallow hard.

"But you know," he begins as his fingers finally touch my skin, clamp around my bicep and pull me close. "That you can never really quit the music." He shrugs and tosses his joint into some bushes behind me. "But the rest of the stuff ... "

I want to tell him; I have to. Not for him, but for me. For that kid he's so obsessed with that doesn't exist anymore, the one that I kind of wish still did.

"Meet me after the show," I say as I make the second hardest decision of my life and step back, drawing my arm from Turner's grip and finding myself icy cold in the middle of all this desert heat. "Meet me after the show and I'll tell you everything."

CHAPTER 14
&TURNER CAMPBELL &

After talking to Naomi, I feel like I'm having an out of body fucking experience, floating above myself and wondering how I've let my life get the way it is. I have the chance and the opportunity to have everything, and yet, I still have nothing. I've had sex with over a hundred girls (I stopped fucking counting a long time ago), but I've never had a girlfriend. Never. Not once. Naomi makes me wonder what I'm missing out on at the same time she pisses me off and makes me see red. She's interesting, that's what it is. I find her so fascinating that I want to grab her and keep hold, make her mine just so I can see what it is she's gonna do next, even if I hate it,

even if it pisses me off. And I don't even know her. I wonder if that has anything to do with it, if maybe after I get to know her that she'll be less interesting. See, the thing is, I have no experience with which to base this shit on.

So I convince myself that maybe I should find out and head back to the bus to slip on a hoodie. I hide in the back of the crowd, and I watch as Amatory Riot heads onstage, letting my eyes follow Naomi in her tight, black tank, her short shorts and her ripped tights. She's got on these steel-toed boots that look like they're meant to stomp the world into shreds, and I can tell that the crowd likes her, maybe even more than that skinny bitch at the mic. What's her name?

I cross my arms over my chest and let a smile slither across my face as Knox slips her guitar over her head and hits it, drawing the crowd – myself included – into the music so fast that it makes their heads spin. She bites her lip and she sweats so hard that she's splattering the crowd with moisture as she flings that axe around and destroys them. And when she does sing, her voice nearly overwhelms Skinny up there, and I know without a doubt that if she wanted to, she could steal the show same way she did when she challenged me.

My smile turns into a fat ass grin as I lean back against the wall and slip my hand down to the waistband

of my pants. It's dark and crowded and sweaty in here, and I guarantee that I'm not the only one doing this. My fingers sneak open the button and fly on my pants, hidden beneath the baggy folds of the sweatshirt. When I finally get a good grip on my cock, a groan escapes me, melting into the collective moans of the crowd as they eat up the music, the words.

"Soaked in your betrayal, drenched with pain and disbelief, I wander. At first I walk, but then I run because I can't stand being here even a second longer. With you. With you. But most especially without you."

I stroke the length of my shaft with strong fingers, using the sweat from my heated body to glide up and down with long, slow strokes, just the way I'd like to do to Naomi. God, I wish I could remember what she felt like beneath me that night, if things would be different if I could remember. *I doubt that, Turner. You would have smiled at her and kissed her goodbye, tossed her a T-shirt and said* have a good life. *Count yourself lucky that you stumbled out of there before she woke up.* I squeeze my dick harder and try to focus on the here and now. Like I said, fuck the past.

Naomi's desert eyes start out dry, but after the first song, they're moist as fuck, lit up by the wetness that leaks down her face and betrays the tight set of her jaw, the straightness of her knees, the screams that burst from

her throat as she riles the crowd into a frenzy so powerful that I get swept away and have to button up my pants, climbing into the mass and getting into the music in a way I haven't been able to for a long, long time.

When she sees me, she knows. Even the hoodie dripping over my face can't keep her from locking gazes with me, from holding me with that stare as I'm shuffled through the crowd, pushed forward by unseen hands. I don't know if it's just chance or fate, but I end up at the front with my body pressed against the metal fence that separates the crowd from the bouncers who guard the stage. Girls press up against me, and for the first time *ever,* I don't really notice them. Right now, Naomi's got my full attention, drowning me in melodic mind fucks and rampaging riffs. I stop being Turner Campbell, frontman for Indecency, and start just *being.* Can't even tell you how good that feels.

"*No, I won't let you ruin me; I won't let you win. Pushing me down only lifted me up, and now I'm here to stay, and it's your turn to feel this way, this broken, bloody, shattered way.*"

There's this charge in the air, and it takes me awhile to get it at first, to really put it all together. It's melancholy.

I never stop to wonder if it has anything to do with me.

By the time I get around back, Milo is having one of his customary panic attacks, pacing back and forth and bitching to anyone that'll listen. When I glance at my phone on the way in, I see that I have several missed calls and a couple of texts. In a jovial fucking mood from watching Naomi, I snap a friendly shot of my ass and message that to him, smiling when I see his face register the photo.

"Miss me?" I ask as I slip into the darkness stage left and toss him a nasty smirk. Milo's blonde hair is sticking up every which way, and his eyes are round as marbles in his pale face. I stare at him for a moment and try not to let him ruin my good mood. "Dude, you need to chill the fuck out."

"Turner," he says, but that's all he can get out because I'm walking on stage and grabbing the mic, pulling the band out behind me without using a single word. That's the way I like it. I lead, and they follow. I've lived too long with life being the other way around, and I'm done with that shit. In fact, today, I don't even pick a girl out in the crowd like usual. I just smile into the mic and say

what I'm feeling. If the crowd doesn't like it, they can go fuck themselves.

"Hey there, Tucson," I growl, and I watch as they ripple with shudders and gasps. *God, I'm on top of the fucking world right now.* Maybe it's a false high, but that's really all anything ever is. Temporary. Fleeting. "I hope you enjoyed Amatory Riot," I say and cheers go up, violent ones, like a horde of howling fucking demons. My eyes flicker to stage right, and there she is, standing there, watching me with those stupid fucking shades on, arms crossed over her tits, sweat sticking her shirt to her skin. "Because I've got a big ass crush on their guitarist." I pause and listen to the collective voice of the room. It stretches out before me into the darkness, eyes and cells winking at me from the balconies, from beneath the chandelier that hangs precariously above them all, heavy and drooping with glass teardrops.

I smile.

"And I'm going to try to fuck her tonight." More cheering, hissing, some whoops. "But first," I continue, eyes sliding to the side. Good sign. Naomi's still standing there; if she hasn't left, good things could be in store for me. I slide the mic out of the stand. "First, I'm going to fuck the shit out of you."

I open my mouth and I take a deep breath, drawing air into my lungs for that first scream, the one that breaks

down the sound barriers and opens up the souls of the people below me. Usually, when I'm up here, all I do is drink in the attention, soak it up like a sponge, revel in the worship. Tonight, my focus is a bit different, and it scares the shit out of me. Yeah, I still like to be looked at, idolized, who doesn't? But there's one person that refuses to participate, and she's the only one tonight that I care about.

"*If you leave me for dead then you're making a mistake again,*" I sing the words, and I try to charge them up with all the sexual tension that I'm feeling in my fucking bones right now. Naomi isn't just under my skin anymore; she's in my blood and my brain and all sorts of strange friggin' places that ache for her. I want to feel her body beneath mine, run my fingers through her hair, taste her lips again. I use my fingers in a subtle cue, invite her onstage with me. Somehow, I guess that if I can recapture that tension we had before, that excitement, that maybe I can breathe easier, better, but when I glance her way again, she's gone.

I suck up my irritation, and I face the crowd again, belting out the next words to the song, wondering why I'm so worked up on this girl and this kid and this weird fairytale fantasy that's been growing in my head ever since I heard her tell me what happened between us.

"*And a mistake made twice isn't really a mistake at*

all."

Naomi Knox is waiting outside my bus when I finish my set, soaked in sweat and ready to tear into her for running off. I don't know why, but something about her makes my emotions go all haywire, like I can't even think when she's around. She fucks up my inner circuits or something. That should have been my first warning, but no, I guess I'm a glutton for punishment.

She's sitting in one of Ronnie's cheap, plastic lawn chairs, smoking a cigarette. I like the way she's bent over, leaning her elbows on her knees, holding the cig between two fingers. She looks tough that way, and I like it.

"Ran off pretty quick there," I tell her as I come up close and lean against the red and black side of the bus. My heart is pounding from the adrenaline rush, and my head's as swollen as it ever gets, full of ego and self and knowledge that no matter what happens, no matter what anyone says, I am the shit. I worked my ass off to get here, and nobody is going to take that fucking away from

me. "I was hoping you'd stick around for my set."

"I had some thinking to do," Naomi says, sitting up, brushing some of her blonde hair behind her ear. It's natural, you know. Kind of a surprise. Not many like that, and I'm speaking from straight-up fucking experience. She puts her cigarette out in the dust near her feet and leans back. I watch a line of sweat drip down her neck and over the tattoo on her chest until it disappears between her breasts.

"Yeah?" I cross my arms over my chest and wait while she stares out and up, presumably gazing at the sky though it's kinda hard to tell with those sunglasses on her face. My guess is that she put 'em on by accident and started to like how they made her feel – protected. The eyes are the windows to the soul and all that shit, right? Guess she wants her windows curtained. "About?"

"You," she says, and I can't help the smirk that crawls across my face when I hear that. She was thinking about little old me? Aw, how fucking sweet. Just the way I like it. "About why you were being so nice to me all of a sudden, flipping the switch from bad boy to concerned father in a single night." My smirk drops into a frown. From the tone of her voice, she's not impressed. Fine. The way I was behaving wasn't an act. If she doesn't like it, she can go fuck herself six ways to Sunday.

And once again, what the fuck is with all the mixed

signals? One minute, she's getting all up close and personal with me in the parking lot, letting me touch her, gazing at me with dilated pupils, licking her lips until they're moist. Now, what, she's annoyed with me again? Jesus Christ, I don't understand this chick at all.

"And I thought, just for a split second mind you, that maybe you had realized the error of your ways. Like, had a revelation or some shit." Naomi sighs and removes her shades, showing me puffy eyes streaked with red, like maybe she didn't stop crying when she got off stage. Right. The melancholy, but how could I have forgotten? Guess whatever it is is my fault, too? "But I should know better," she continues, staring at me with eyes so bright that I can't look away, not even with a stray fangirl shouts for me to look at her, snaps a picture with an old Polaroid camera. I don't even look when the bouncer comes to drag her away. Neither does Naomi. "People don't change overnight." She pauses, smiles. In this light, I can see that her straight nose isn't actually all that straight, that in reality, when the light hits it right, it's a bit crooked. *Fuck, Turner, since when do you care about women's noses? That's fucking weird, dude.*

"Oh? And finding out I had a kid didn't change me in the few seconds it took my brain to process that information? Oh, honey, if you were waiting for an overnight change, then you were waiting far too long.

The second those words left your lips, I was a different man."

Naomi laughs and shakes her head which just further pisses me off. Who the fuck does she think she is? She joins *my* tour, disrespects me, turns my life upside down, and then proceeds to fuck with me. Bitch has a lot of nerve.

But I'm still interested.

Either I'm a glutton for punishment or the drugs really have done what the PA's always said they'd do, and rotted my fucking brain right out of my skull.

"Is that so hard to believe, Knox?" I ask her and notice that her lips purse tight when I use her last name. I wonder why she hates it so much.

Naomi touches her fingers to the tattoo on her belly, the one that's peeking out from beneath her shirt right now. I can't see what it says from here, but I see a set of angel wings on either side, so maybe it's something good? Our kid's name? I don't know, but I lean forward to get a better look.

"It's hard to believe, Turner, because as soon as I tell you the truth, the whole, unabridged version of the truth, I know exactly what it is you're going to do." She pauses again and bites her lower lip hard when Ronnie and Treyjan stumble around the front of the bus and see us there. I turn and flash them my worst *do not fuck this*

shit up glare, and have to admit that I'm pleased when they leave without a fight. I'm still the boss around here, good to know. "My guess is that I've helped you in some weird, kind of fucked up way. Part of me knows that you'll work to make your fantasy happen, no matter how you have to go about doing it."

"My fantasy? What the fuck are you smoking, Naomi? I just want to know about my kid." *Not entirely true, but she's obviously not up for anything else tonight.* That much is obvious. No matter. I'll get the kid, and I'll get the mother. It's a fact of life. Whatever she says to the contrary, anything about not wanting to see the child or how its adoptive family might act, I know she's in pain. It's etched into every line of her face, every word she speaks, every breath she breathes.

"You've somehow got it into your mind that there's going to be this big ass fucking reunion with some miracle child who will just throw themselves into your arms and shout, *Daddy!*" Naomi stands up suddenly and throws her arms in the air. "That they'll just come away with you, and I'll follow, that you'll have the family you've always wanted. Am I right, Turner?" She smiles wickedly at me. "Tell me I'm right about that."

I stare right back at her, and I think about what she's saying. Is that what I'm doing? Trying to put together a family all of a sudden? Maybe. I try not to delve too

deep into thoughts like that, but yeah. Yeah. Sure.

I tell her the truth. After all, it's my fucking policy.

"What's wrong with that?" I take a step closer to her, wondering how far she'll let me go before she runs away again. I lock my eyes with hers and wait for the answer to the question.

"From whore to family man in just a matter of days?" she asks this sarcastically, and I get the feeling she's actually trying to rile me up. Doesn't work. I cross my arms over my chest and tilt my chin back.

"A kid changes everything. Most people have time to get used to this shit. You just sprung it on me. What do you want me to do? I have a six year old running around out there somewhere that I've never met. You know how fucked up that is?"

"Turner," Naomi says, shaking her head like she can't believe what it is she's about to say. "There is no – "

"Naomi!" A voice cuts through our conversation and a second later, pretty boy emo fag Dax is standing behind her panting. In his eyes, I can see that he thinks he's in love with her, and it makes me sick. I don't know exactly what it is that I want from her, but she's right – a family might be it – so I don't like the idea of Dax moving in on what's mine. Pisses me the fuck off.

"What?" she snaps, and I'm glad to see her taking her anger out on him, too. Dax looks at her carefully and

speaks very, very slowly.

"Naomi, the police are here, and they're looking for you."

CHAPTER 15
❦ NAOMI KNOX ❦

Aw, shit.

My mind starts to spin as soon as Dax's lips utter the word police, and then I'm thinking about my other big secret and the dirty mess I made back in Tulsa. The one that was videotaped without my ever knowing it. The one that's sitting on America's iPad ready to be seen by anyone that has access to it. God, I hope she was smart and finally deleted that thing. Strange that it never occurred to me to ask. I've never been good at subterfuge. Jesus and fuck and fuck and FUCK.

Inside, I freak the fuck out. On the outside, I remain cool as a goddamn cucumber.

"Why?" The word doesn't come from me; it comes

from Turner Campbell. Dax keeps his gaze on my face, but answers the question. He's still wearing the same clothes he had on onstage which is rare for him — normally he makes a flat out sprint to the shower. It's kind of his after show ritual. They must've been waiting for me at the bus.

"They say they're looking for someone." Dax pauses and scratches the dark stubble on his chin. I try not to compare him and Turner because that would imply that I'm interested in one or both of them, and I'm not, but it happens anyway, and I decide that Turner has a better chin. It's thicker, more square, but not barbaric. *Fuck.* My teenage crush on him has come back raging harder than ever, despite the fact that I've already tasted what he had to offer and didn't find it all that great. Plus, he left me knocked up. Not a good way to start a relationship. *Turner and I will never, ever happen. I'd rather die first.*

"Who?" Me, this time, asking as if I don't have a care in the world when in all reality, I have two. Two really, really big cares. Felonies actually. I mean, I haven't been charged with them, but why would the police be here looking for me if it wasn't about that? I didn't stab anyone … Well, not recently anyway.

"Your … brother," Dax says, and my heart plummets to the dirt beneath my feet. Shit. Dax licks his lips and looks down at the ground with his gray eyes, like two

gravestones right there on his face, all the contemplative quiet of the dead right in two round orbs. Doesn't hurt that he has them tattooed all over his arms, two full sleeves of dead people and dead things – ghosts, skeletons, zombies. I try to swallow but my mouth is dry as this fucking desert. "I didn't know you had a brother," Dax continues, and his voice sounds kind of hurt though I'm not sure why.

I listen to the sound of the kids leaving in their shitty clunkers, shouting at one another because their ears are too fucked up from the bass to hear anything otherwise. They're sporting our tees and slapping our band stickers on their bumpers, and they think we're just so fucking cool and amazing and carefree, and they have no idea how much shit all of us are in. Being a 'rock star' really just means someone that makes music that fucks up a lot. It's true. Check it in the dictionary.

"I don't." My words are calm, emotionless. I want to slip the shades back on, but I'm starting to think I'm using them as a way to hide. And I don't hide. I might fight or I might run because at least with those two options, I'm making a conscious choice. But hiding? It's like waiting around for someone else to make a decision for you. I don't like that. The secrets are bad enough. I try not to look at Turner during this exchange. I was *just* about to tell him the rest of the secret, just about to clear up this

last, little thing and finally be able to wipe this shit from my mental board of things to do. How come bad stuff always seems to happen all at once?

"Oh." Dax pinches at the front of his green and black striped shirt and looks confused. "But they said they were looking for an – "

"Eric Rhineback?" I ask, and then I take out a cigarette and start walking. Both boys follow me like lost, little puppy dogs. Well, Dax is kind of like a puppy dog; Turner is more like a tramp in heat, searching for a nice, warm bitch. My lip curls. "He was the son of the last foster parents that I had." I shrug and continue on, rounding the end of the bus and heading straight towards the pair of people in blue uniforms. "Though I'd hardly call him a brother."

"Why would they come here looking for him?" Dax asks, making me wonder that very same thing. Why indeed. I don't answer that question, because I can't and instead pick up the pace, so I can get this over with and switch back to Turner and our little problem.

"Naomi Knox?" one of the police asks as I step up close and flash my ID. I don't even answer the question verbally, just flick my cigarette at them. The male officer, this big, fat dude with a mustache, tries to smile at me, while his female partner glares at me from behind her blonde dike cut. Overcompensating much?

"What?" I snap because, well, the best way to make yourself look innocent is to act like you could give a rat's ass less about what's going on. I tap the ash of my cigarette onto the guy's shoe. Behind me, I hear Turner and Dax settling in to watch. Obviously, I'm not going to be getting rid of either of them yet. The male officer squints at me like he doesn't quite understand my behavior. I don't smile or apologize.

"Miss Knox, we're here looking to find out if you've had any contact with Eric Rhineback." Already, I'm shaking my head. I drop my cig to the ground and put it out with the steel toe of my boot. All around us, people are scurrying to avoid the eyes of the cops, putting halts on their drug deals and switching out joints for cigarettes.

"I haven't talked to Eric since the investigation," I tell them, trying to forget what is probably the worst memory I've got next to the whole Turner-baby thing. The angst, the anxiety, the stomach aches. Ugh. If I had to go back to that again, I'd kill myself. When the whole stabbing incident occurred, I almost did. Being scrutinized and torn apart by law enforcement sucks. I mean, I get that they're trying to do their jobs, but shit, the pressure sucks. "Why would he be here? I'm on tour. We barely stay in one place for a day."

The male cop nods like he was expecting me to say this, but the female cop is glaring at me and stepping

forward like she really, really wants to find some excuse to nail me right now. I stretch my arms above my head and lock my hands together.

"He's wanted for the murder of Chuck and McKenzie Rhineback."

I stare at them both and try not to betray my feelings with my face. I used to be real good at that, but Turner keeps sniffing me out, so I don't know, maybe I'm starting to lose it.

"Oh?" I ask, trying to sound surprised. "I thought he'd been cleared as a suspect?" Okay, yeah, I'm fishing for information, but who wouldn't in this scenario. The female cop smiles but avoids my question.

"Well, if you think of anything, you give us a call. His car was spotted on the interstate day before yesterday by one of our patrols. We looked up friends and family that might be in the area, and you're the only possibility that popped up."

I scowl.

"Yeah, well, I'm no friend of Eric Rhineback's." I shrug and try to ignore the questioning eyes that are burning into my back *and* front. America is staring at me like I'm about to get a big, fat spanking and get sent to my room without dessert; Turner and Dax are burning me up with questions, and I can't even see them. Jesus. Now, I just want to go to bed. I'd been planning on dropping

some acid, but the last thing I need right now is to end up running down the street buck naked thinking the devil's about to stab me with a pitchfork. The LSD will do that to you, you know. Sensing that my answer wasn't enough, I add, "But I'll call you if he shows up." I think of my phone. "I no longer have a mobile device, so if you're wanting my cell records … "

"No need for anything as drastic as that," says Mustache Cop. "Just be careful. The guy … " He pauses and looks into my eyes with moist, nervous ones, like he's imagining the crime photos. They're pretty gruesome; once you see them, you don't forget. "He's a psychopath and a murderer." I nod and watch as America oozes down the steps and schmoozes the shit out of the officers, using her good manners to pick up where my bad ones left off. In her white suit and red heels, she looks like a force to be reckoned with. Good. Maybe they'll think twice before coming out here again.

I turn around and glance at Dax and Turner. I should finish my conversation, but I'm just not in the mood anymore. Like I said, one secret at a time is all I can handle and right now, I can't decide whether to be happy or sad. After all, I've just been questioned about a guy who's getting charged with a crime he didn't commit. And I know that for a fact.

Since I'm the one that committed it.

I light another cigarette and turn around without another word, disappearing onto the bus with only my thoughts for company.

The next morning when I wake up, the first words out of my mouth are, "The video?"

America doesn't even look up at me, keeping her eyes on the Facebook page she's perusing, making sure there are no nasty comments left for us, no negative reviews, no perverts. America likes to make dirty things clean. Good for her.

"Do you honestly even need to ask that question?" she says as I stare at the back of her neck, at the freckles that crawl out of her shirt and into her hair. I look at them for awhile and then pop the top on a can of beer. I don't tell her thank you or anything like that, just turn around and start back towards the shower.

Hayden beats me to it and tosses her dirty tank from last night at my head. I bat it away with a growl and narrow my eyes. She's standing naked and proud in front of me, arms crossed under her small breasts, and doesn't

even give a shit that Kash is watching her from his place on the bunk next to me.

"Heard about your troubles last night," she says and I come *this* close to punching her in the nose. She has a small one that's sort of upturned with tiny nostrils that float too high above her thin lips. If I were gay, I'd much rather fuck Blair than Hayden. I reach into my bunk and pull a box of cigs out from beneath my pillow. Not responding to Hayden is probably the best thing I can do. After all, she's the one I told everything to back then, the one that encouraged me, the one that watched from the closet and absorbed my secret, ate it up and saved it for later, so she could throw it up in my face. God, I can't even believe we used to be friends.

"And?" I ask, trying to sound bored. If she knows I'm annoyed with her, she'll get worse. Always does. At least she doesn't know *that* secret, the Turner one. She has no idea that we ever slept together, that I was ever pregnant. Thank God. The bitch is bad enough with one secret under her belt; two would kill me. Or her. Yeah, probably her. Not that I like to make a habit of it. In fact, murder is sort of something I'd never like to repeat. The blood doesn't just stain the hands; it stains the soul, too.

"Seems like you might want to be extra nice to me right now, don't you think?" I stare at her, but I don't say anything. She swipes some hazelnut hair over her

shoulder and gazes at me with the big Bambi eyes that make men (and women) go nuts. Hayden nibbles her lower lip. "I mean, I'm just saying, the cops left a card and said to call them if anything came up. Since they're investigating a murder, I thought maybe – "

I cut her off by flicking cigarette ashes at her feet.

"Fine. I get your point. What do you want now?" When Hayden smiles, slow and wicked as sin, I know I'm in trouble. Whatever it is she's going to say is going to push me over the edge and into the frothing waters of hell. Fuck.

"Turner." That's it, nice and simple. Kash grunts and pulls his curtain up, giving us some semblance of privacy. Can't say I blame him. He hates Turner; every guy here hates him. It's just a simple fact of life on the road with Indecency. He probably hears chicks arguing over Turner Campbell a dozen times a day. You know those fucking horrible T-shirts? The ones that say *Mrs. So-and-so?* Well, Indecency's merch stand sells tanks with Mrs. Campbell on them. Get the point?

My answer, short and just as simple. "No."

She leans back and looks me up and down, sizing me up although she knows good and well how far she can push me. She's been doing it for years, ever since we got Amatory Riot together. I should've never gone back to Tulsa, shoulda kept running and held my head low.

"Oh?" I can't explain my answer to her because I can't explain it to myself either. I could give her Turner. I mean, all I need to do is spend five more minutes with the man, let the cat out of the bag, and watch him shift gears real, real fast. Instead, I just stand there and smoke my cigarette. Gray swirls fill the small space, get caught against the black curtains that cover the bunk beds and sneak into the open door of the bathroom. "Really? Tasted something you liked?" I look at her, and all I can think about is Hayden and Turner fucking, and then I just want to hit something *hard*. I keep my fingers relaxed and my face stoic.

"I won't try to stop you if you're going to pursue him," I tell her, and that's the God honest truth. I won't. Why bother? Even if I was interested (which I'm not), then blocking Hayden wouldn't do me any good. Turner has to learn to say no to temptation or that fantasy family he's dreaming about will never happen. He's weak willed, I think. That's his problem. He wants and wants and wants, and he gets so much that he's never figured out how to just say no. "But I'm kind of working some shit out, and he's a part of it."

Hayden's blue eyes go wide and she crosses her arms behind her head, giving me a full body shot of her curvy figure, her trim waist, the little rose tattoo under her belly button. Even with me, she can't help herself. She has to

flirt and flaunt because that's what she does best. Sometimes, I almost feel sorry for her.

"So he knows?"

"Goddamn it, Hayden," I snarl, letting my temper slip a little. "Of course he doesn't." She laughs, and the sound isn't pleasant, not in the least.

"Then you won't have a problem handing him over?" I make a face at her and cross one arm over my chest.

"Hand him over?" I say, disturbed that she even thinks I have that ability. "To hand him over, I'd have to have some sort of claim over the guy, and I can assure you that I do not. You want me to play handmaiden for you? Fine. I'll cut your steak into little pieces and wipe your ass, but if it's Turner you want, you'll have to figure out a way to get him yourself. Grow some balls, Hayden, and do your own dirty work." I reach under the waistband of my jeans and snap my thong at her, spinning away without another word and storming into the front of the bus, frustrated that we're on the move.

I run my hand through my air and take a deep breath. *One thing at a time,* I tell myself, wondering if Eric really is going to get pinned with his parents' murder. It would be a load off my shoulders, that's for sure, and I wouldn't even feel all that guilty about it. He knew what was going on with his sister, and he didn't do a damn thing to stop it. I did. That was me. And if I had to make the

choice again, I'd still do it. A good person escaped that situation and two bad ones died. Me, I consider myself a neutral, so I guess I'm still in the gray. I wonder if there will ever be a tipping point for me.

Thirty seconds later, I remember the date and my mouth goes dry and my throat closes up.

March 15th.

Shit. I was so preoccupied with secret number one that I forgot about … My stomach churns like crazy and my hands start to shake. Happens to me every year. I get overwhelmed with could-haves and might-have-beens and my whole life starts to seem like one big fraud, like I'm not really living it, like I'm just existing. And it's not just the baby, and it's not just Turner. It's everything. Just everything.

"Dax," I say, and he snaps to attention like a shoulder. I realize then and there that he's really into me. It's hitting him hard, I see. Where before he tried to play it casual, now he's up in arms. He rises to his feet and takes a step towards me. When I spin to face him, I don't smile. Don't want him getting any ideas. "Can I borrow your phone?"

He frowns.

"To call Turner?"

"Does it fucking matter?" I snap at him, and snatch the phone away violently when he hands it over. I storm

into the back, not caring that I'm probably waking Blair and Wren, and step into the second bathroom, plopping my ass down on the toilet lid. It's only then that I realize I don't have his number. That it was blocked, unlisted. Jesus Christ.

I slam the screen of the phone into my forehead, and let the empty beer can fall to the floor at my feet. Reaching behind me, I flush the toilet to get some privacy and practice the words that are floating around inside my skull. When we get to Reno, I want to make sure that I'll still be able to say them.

"Turner," I begin, and I glance up sharply, seeing my reflection pale and frustrated in the mirror that hangs from the back of the door. My eyes are huge, not scared, but nervous maybe. Just a little bit. The question isn't why, because I know that answer somewhere, deep down. It's how come? How can I still be into Turner? How can I still care what he thinks about me or what he has to say? How? How? How? "Turner," I start again, and I don't let my voice get dry or crack, don't let my emotions break through the perfect mask I've plastered over my face. "Turner, there is no kid because there was no baby. Six years ago to the day, I had an abortion."

I spend the rest of the day moping around the bus, tapping my index finger to my lips, nursing a six-pack and an entire carton of cigs. Dax offered me some stronger stuff, but I don't think it'll help. Somehow, I imagine that any advanced narcotics I choose to partake in will only exemplify the feelings churning in my gut. Right now, I need to deal, and I need to do it with as little help as is humanly possible. I have to figure out how to get through this.

See, this abortion is both a big issue and a nonissue for me. Do I regret it? Hell no. Do I feel remorse about it? Fuck yeah. And I blame Turner. I blame him for leaving me alone with a decision I wasn't ready to make at all, let alone by myself. I blame him for seducing me, for preying on my infatuation with him. And the whole condom thing? Yeah, maybe I should of checked, but I was losing my V card to a rock star, and I was not quite seventeen, and he, he was the one that should have taken care of that.

I crush my empty beer can in one hand and toss it into the trash. Seconds later, Blair rescues it and moves it to

the recycling bin. I ignore her. I ignore everyone, even America when she starts to bitch about practice and how lax we've all been. Fuck, she should just be glad I'm even functioning at all. Last year, I just laid in bed and watched Indecency music videos. Yup, I'm a glutton for punishment.

I crack the top of my next drink and try not to imagine what it would be like to have a six year old right now. I figure that it'd be just like it is now: a perfect blend of heaven and hell. Life likes to be balanced, you know? Things can't all be rosy and cheerful. I smoke my cigarette and pace back down to the end of the bus, pausing to glance out the windows on either side.

As the highway flashes by in stretches of pavement and metal, I think about how I felt when I pissed on that goddamn stick way back when. Adoption was never an option for me. Call me selfish, but it was my way or the highway. Maybe that's because I know firsthand what it's like to be adopted – or not. If I put someone in this world who had to experience even half the shit I did, I'd never forgive myself. So yeah, I guess I know where Turner's coming from. I wonder then, how he'll feel when he finds out. I want to believe that that arrogant, cocky, son of a bitch will be happy, glad he's free of baggage, but I know otherwise. Turner *wanted* that kid. Why? I have no fucking clue. To put together a perfect fantasy family?

To soothe his own insecurities and shortcomings?

"He should just go knock up one of his groupie bitches," I whisper under my breath, pressing my forehead to the glass of the window and letting my lashes kiss my reflection. I don't think what I did was wrong: I was seventeen, pregnant, homeless. And my hands were covered in blood, both literally and figuratively.

I killed my foster parents. Both of them. While they were sleeping. Some mother I'd have made.

I think that's what makes this day hurt so much. I lost a possibility, a chance at something different, because I was too damaged to even give it a shot. My birth parents, whoever the shit they were, fucked me; my adoptive parents screwed me; the foster system destroyed me. And Turner? He was just icing on the friggin' cake, baby.

I remind myself that that's why I'm here, why I'm doing this. I came on this tour because I wanted to make a life for myself. I didn't let Turner's presence scare me away then; I won't let it bother me now. I need to do what's right for me, what'll make me feel better, and right now, I just want this secret to go away. I don't want to carry it any longer, and I don't want March 15th to mean a damn thing other than the day I finally broke free of one set of chains.

I check my watch and smile.

Just enough time left to pretty up.

CHAPTER 16
TURNER CAMPBELL

After the police thing with Naomi, I'm even more interested in her. Even coming back to the bus to find that Ronnie and Treyjan had invited a girl into my bed hadn't done it for me. We'd fooled around for a bit, but I didn't fuck her. Told her I was tired and she stormed out after a massive sobbing fit that woke everybody on the damn bus. Fine. Her loss.

I slide some gel through the back of my hair, letting it stick out in all directions – messy, unassuming. But carefully planned. Perfect. Eyeliner goes around my eyes, not enough to look like some kind of emo fuck, but just enough that my eyes are haunted, far away. I change out the stud in my tongue, switch out the piercings on

either side of my lip for rings, and slip red plugs into my earlobes.

"Primping for Miss Naomi Knox?" Treyjan asks, leaning around the edge of the door frame and flicking his tongue out at me. His brown hair is sticking straight up and he's got a tie around his neck, but no shirt. Typical Trey. I grin at myself in the mirror and give him a look over my shoulder.

"I might be. What's it to you? You interested?" Treyjan shrugs his shoulder and starts digging around in his jeans pockets for a smoke.

"I wasn't until I saw her running naked across the parking lot the other night. Damn, girl's got a body." I try to ignore the fact that my hands curl at my sides and the air gets a hell of a lot thicker. I smirk and run my fingers through my hair once last time, just to make sure it's perfect.

"Yeah, we had a bit of a thing," I tell him, refusing to elaborate. If he knows Naomi and I didn't have sex that night, he doesn't let on.

"I can see that," he tells me as he moves back and makes room for me to step past him and start towards the door. We've been parked for about an hour now, and I'm tired of waiting. I want to see Naomi. No, maybe that's not it. I *need* to see her, and I need to find my kid. "But why? A few days ago, you acted like you couldn't stand

her. Now you're in love or some shit? What's going on, Turner? I've known you a long ass time now, and I've never seen you look at a girl the way you look at her." I pause with my foot on the top step, ready to descend. Part of me wants to break down and have some sort of gay ass heart to heart with Trey, tell him everything.

Instead I say, "Hey Treyjan, what are you named after again? Oh yeah, that thing that failed and got your mommy preggers with you." I reach into my back pocket and grab a Trojan, tossing the little square package over my shoulder as I step out and onto the cement.

"Hey Turner," he shouts after me. "Fuck you, dude." And then for a few blissful moments there, everything is normal. Better than normal even. And then I run into Naomi, and a smile curls across my lips. My body goes crazy and my heart starts to pump.

She looks fucking perfect tonight, dressed in a white, sleeveless button up that isn't actually buttoned, just pinned together over her chest with an Amatory Riot button. The teal color of their logo only emphasizes the matching bra beneath, the one that peeks out at me as she moves. Around her neck is a black tie with a skull on it, made out of the same fabric as the very, very, very short fucking mini skirt she's got on.

She pauses in front of me and places her hands on her hips, letting out a sigh that I don't quite get.

"Hey there, sexy," I say, and I can't help but notice the way her lip curls up at the edge. There's still heat between us, so much so that my dick is already hard and my body is starting to sweat. I find myself licking my lips and running my hand through my hair. And she, she just stands there and looks at me with eyes so shadowed in secrets that I can't even tell what color they are anymore. "You know," I begin before she can say anything. "It's true. Honesty really is the best fucking policy. You had something you wanted to tell me?" She lets her mouth twist into an all out sneer and steps back, shaking her head like she can't even believe I just said that. "It'll clear your head, I promise."

"Oh really?" she asks sarcastically. "You have no idea what it'll do for me, so don't even bother making false proclamations." Naomi holds up her palms to pause the next words that are about to come out of my mouth. "Let me just get this out, so we can be done with each other, alright?" I raise my eyebrows and click my tongue stud against my teeth.

"Done with each other?" I ask, taking a step forward, clasping Naomi tight around the upper arms. As soon as our skin makes contact with one another, it's like a bomb going off, exploding my brain into mush, shrinking me down to nothing, pushing me forward. "But I'm just getting started." My mouth captures hers and tastes hot

heat and cigarettes, dragging a moan from my throat that gets lost in a desperate frenzy of clawing fingers and gnashing teeth. Naomi and I, we kiss hard and rough, like we're not just trying to make out, but like we're trying to hurt each other, too. I don't quite get the feelings that are running through my blood, tangling my fingers in her hair, pressing her face to mine.

I have to say, when she hits me in the stomach and steps back, I'm not surprised. Saliva shimmers on her full lips and makes them seem all the more appealing. My mouth waters in response as I take a hand to my lips and wipe away the spit.

"Fuck, what is it now?" I ask her and for the first time, I see this hint of vulnerability, this trickle of uncertainty flutter across her face and then it's gone like it never was. I life my hands up and cross them behind my head, letting my eyes close, so I won't get pissed. I want to scream at her, ask her what her problem is. Despite what she might think, I'm not invincible. Certain things set me off, and getting hit is one of them. I got hit enough by my mom and step daddies. Getting wailed on again is not an option. Only her. I only let her do it, and I don't know why.

"Turner, there is no kid," she blurts and my eyes open quickly, fix her with a tight stare.

"What?" My first thought is that she fucking lied to

me. The thought makes me crazy, so crazy that I almost turn around and walk away. I've had girls play the pregnancy card before, say that the condom didn't work or some shit. They were all liars, eventually copped to the fact that they were just trying to trap me. I don't want to be trapped. I want to be enraptured. Naomi does that to me, and when she told me, I could tell she wasn't saying the words to get a reaction out of me. She was speaking to empty herself. How could what she said have been a lie? How? I blink and my mouth curls dangerously. The muscles in my arms twitch.

Naomi runs her hand through her hair and pulls out a lighter, snapping it open and jamming a cigarette between her teeth. She's shaking, just a little, but whether with anger or excitement or fear, I have no clue.

"There is no kid, Turner. Not anymore." She snaps her eyes to mine, dares me to defy her with that dry, desert gaze. I drop my arms to my sides.

"I don't follow."

She barks out a bit of harsh laughter and shakes her head, stepping back and putting her hands on her lower back, bending over so that she's facing the ground and not me.

"Of course you don't," I hear her whisper, and then my anger gets the better of me, and I'm stepping forward and pushing her back. She stumbles a bit and then recovers,

launching herself at me and decking me under the chin with a hard right upper cut that makes my teeth hurt and forces me back a step or two.

"My kid is dead?" I ask and then she starts to laugh, crazy laugh, like so loud that people start to stare. "He's dead and you're laughing?"

I hear footsteps and I know people are coming to break up the fight that we're only sort of having.

"My kid," she repeats, pulling herself up straight, filling her lungs with air. "It was my kid and my choice to make. You hold no rights to that memory, Turner. The only reason I'm even telling you this is because I'm tired of being haunted by all these ghosts." Naomi gestures violently at the air around her. "I'm tired of counting down the time to this day, this day that six years ago I had the abortion. It shouldn't bother me anymore, but it does. It does, and you know why, Turner?" She points at me and then holds up her other hand to stop Dax from bursting into the mix. He's followed closely by their skinny bitch singer; I hear Trey pause behind me. "It bothers me because I let myself get tangled up in you. I fell in love with an image, a false idol beaming down at me from on high, and right after I lost everything – my dignity, my morals, my sense of self – you took all that was left. You may not have meant to, and it may not have been personal, but that just makes it worse. You brought me to my knees without knowing you were doing it, not even caring. You meant the world to me, and I meant nothing to you. Well, you know what? I'm not a teenager anymore, and I don't look up to you. I don't respect you, and honestly, I think you're one of the most despicable creatures to ever grace this earth." Naomi stands tall and for a second there, I think she's going to cry, but she doesn't. Naomi Knox holds her head high and spills one of her festering, rotten secrets into the air. I hope it makes her feel better to talk to me like that, get all these things off her chest, because it makes me sick.

My head starts to spin, and I feel dizzy.

"Naomi," I start, but she interrupts me.

"Just over six years ago, you stepped in and helped me out, and then we spent a night together that I will never forget." Naomi reaches behind her back and comes up with a knife. I take a step back and Dax moves in close, but she isn't coming after me. Instead, she bends down and unzips her boot, revealing a bare calf and ankle underneath. The tattoo of my name winks back at me. "You left me with a full belly and an empty heart," she says with a sigh. "And you still had power over me because I let you." Naomi pauses. "Not anymore. The cat's out of the bag and about to get skinned."

The knife flashes down and slices skin, cuts right down the side of that little heart tattoo, and before I know

it, I'm moving forward and shoving Dax back, sliding to my knees in the dirt and cupping Naomi under the chin with my hands. I don't try to take away the knife because that isn't my fucking choice to make, but I look her in the eyes and I don't know what to say. My chest and throat get tight, and I feel something there, bubbling beneath the angry, but I'm upset and I'm only thinking of myself. What's new?

All I can think is that she was right: I was looking for some kind of fantasy family. What the shit was I thinking? And she lead me on. Sort of. Or maybe I just jumped to conclusions all on my own … I can't even keep my mind straight right now. Instead of coming up with something meaningful, I just kiss her which is so totally out of place for the moment that I don't even blame her when the knife comes up and slashes my arm, mixes my blood with hers.

Naomi drops the knife and scrambles backward, lurching to her feet and stumbling out of there with blood trailing behind her, beading on the dusty cement in crimson dots.

CHAPTER 17
& NAOMI KNOX &

How do you live down a scene like that? Hmm? How do
you walk away knowing that everybody thinks you're a
friggin' psychopath? And maybe I am, just a little. For a
second, I lost it there, but now that I'm standing on the
stage with my ankle throbbing and my axe pressed
against my crotch, I feel a whole lot better.

One secret down, one to go.

I slam my pick down hard, squat into the guitar, meet
Wren for a little back to back rendezvous center stage.
This, this is where I was always meant to be – drowning
in music and sweat and blood. The stage is my life now,
and the day I forget that, I'm royally screwed. I don't
need Turner or the ghost of that baby or anything like

that. Me and my Wolfgang, me and my music. That's all there has to be.

So I rock hard, and then I run away, retreating to the safety of the bus without seeing Turner. Somehow, like by magic, Dax is there waiting for me. The softness in his gray eyes scares the shit out of me and tells me that he's about to admit it, to me and to himself. Dax has a thing for me. Fuck.

"Dax, I can't do this right now," I tell him when his lips part and he starts to speak. I put my hand on the counter to steady myself. I don't want a confession of undying love right now. I don't want love at all. I don't understand it, and it scares the ever living shit out of me.

Dax blinks a few times like he isn't sure what to make of my words. We're both soaked in sweat and tired, shaking from the rush of adrenaline that performing always brings up. I just want to shower and sleep. Or just sleep. Maybe just that.

"Naomi, I … "

"Dax, I'm fucking serious!" I scream at him, and I don't feel guilty, not even a little bit, not even when his face falls and his eyes darken. Dax looks at me for a long moment, one that seems to stretch into eternity. I don't move. I can't right now. When he finally just nods and moves away, all I feel is relief.

My hands start to shake, and I find myself suddenly

desperate for empty attention, like a sex addict or something. I think of this book I read once where the main character fucked people to feel whole inside. I get it, sort of, I do. But I don't need to feel whole. Right now, I'm practically bursting with emotion. I want to feel empty.

So I descend the stairs of the bus and go off in search of a partner.

What I find instead is my long, lost foster brother. Eric Rhineback.

"What do you want?" First words out of my mouth.

Eric smiles a smile that's so like his father's that I feel sick. He's standing about six feet away from me, dressed in a fancy suit, like he's somebody. I call bullshit. Eric is just a nobody with a trailer of false hope being towed behind him.

"Good to see you, too, Naomi." Eric moves forward and extends his hand. I don't move away from his advance, but I also refuse to shake with him. If I touch him, in even the smallest way, I may kill him.

"Cops are looking for you." I light up and blow smoke out through my teeth, examining the dark suit and the way it's tailored perfectly to his body. Must've cost a lot of money, that thing. I wonder where he got it from. Eric drops his thin, pale hand and licks his lips. "Apparently, they think you killed your parents."

"Strange that, isn't it?" he asks, dark hair so clean and polished that it glistens, even with only the dim lights from the street nearby. Music trickles out of the building, shouting, screaming. Turner's onstage right now, singing his heart out, spreading his angel wings so wide that they obscure his devil tail. "Since supposedly you and I got rid of the evidence. I wonder how they got it into their heads that it was me." I stare at him and take a drag on my cig.

"You're blaming me for this?" I ask him, incredulous. Eric shrugs and the movement is just as easy and carefree now as it was back then, when he was young and I was younger, when I thought he walked on water and shit. Good thing I learned quick that that wasn't true. "I'm not involved in any of this." I pause as a thought hits me. "Did you send it?" I ask him, being purposefully vague. Eric looks at me like I'm nuts.

"You think I'd mail the cops the murder weapon? With my fingerprints on it? Wow, you really have lost it."

"Murder weapon?" I ask, thinking of the bloodstained scissors, the way they felt in my hand when I plunged them into that rapist's throat. "They can't possibly have the murder weapon."

"Why not?" Eric asks, but I'm hardly listening.

"Because I do." *Okay, so he obviously doesn't know what I'm talking about. If he did send the video, then he's doing a damn good job of hiding it.* "And the birds," I continue, curious to see his reaction. Again, I get the crazy person look.

"What the fuck are you blabbering about, Naomi?" he hisses, leaning forward, blue eyes winking back at me, shiny with fear. "I don't know anything about fucking birds. What I do know is that the cops are convinced that it was me. Are you sure you still have the scissors? If you do, then I'll know they're bluffing. If not … "

"If not, what?" I ask him, heart pounding furiously. I don't know why. Eric doesn't know it was me. In fact, he's thoroughly convinced that it was his sister. And he's never blamed her. All he's ever done is try to cover this up, brush it under the rug. He knows what they did to her, but he never tried to stop it. I wonder if he thinks cleaning up some blood redeems him for that.

"Shit, I don't know," he snarls. "Things are going good for me, Naomi. I can't have this screw it up."

"So you came looking for me?"

"Yes!" He throws up his hands and then pinches his thin lips together. "Katie is missing." My heart skips a beat, starts up again at a galloping pace.

"Missing?"

"Yeah, as in gone. I can't find her anywhere, and Naomi, it's gotten worse." I swallow hard.

"It has?"

"Yeah. So bad that she was committed." Eric pauses and tucks his hands into his pockets. When the right one escapes, it's clasped around a silver flask. He tips it to his lips and drinks deep. Reminds me of the nights we used to spend looking at the stars and getting plastered. I used to think he took me out there because he liked me. In reality, he just didn't want to hear what was happening to his sister.

I take it and swallow big. If Katie is missing, then I have my answers. Not for sure maybe, but probably. It would explain a lot.

"Come on," I say, turning away slightly and motioning for Eric to follow me. "Let's go find those scissors."

They're gone, of course. Six years of carrying them around in the bottom of the purse I never use and suddenly, they're just missing. I sit on the floor with my legs bent at the knee, feet trailing behind me. Useless items sprawl everywhere in the tiny space – gum wrappers, tubes of lipstick, an old cell phone that doesn't work anymore held together with tape.

Eric is gone; he had no choice. Dax was still in the shower when we got back, but America was sitting at the table in front. I sent him away with a promise to call if I found the scissors. He gave me a business card and left. It's sitting next to my right knee now, under a box of gold thumbtacks.

Katie Rhineback.

I can't blame her for the problems she has; one time, her mother locked her in a closet for a week with two water bottles – one full of orange juice to drink, the other to piss in. She was ten at the time. I rub my hands over my face and I remind myself that it was worth it, that the Rhinebacks were miserable excuses for human beings. They had to die for what they did to Katie, for what they tried to do to me, for what they could've and would've done to many others.

"Fuck."

"Everything okay?"

The voice to my right scares the shit out of me and

makes me jump. But it's just Dax. I ignore him and start shoveling the items together, pushing them in the purse and out of sight. Back they go in the drawer beneath my bunk. I have to keep my shit there or Spencer fucks with it when she cleans. I stand up just in time to see Hayden appear from behind Dax like a ghost, all pale and sweaty, fucked up as shit.

She stumbles forward and catches herself on Dax's shoulder, gigging raucously, letting her tits fall out of the tight, black corset she donned for tonight's show. Dax's face shows no irritation, just concern as he helps Hayden find her feet and lets her throw herself into his arms. As she kisses his neck, he looks straight over her shoulder at me.

"I don't want to talk right now," I tell him, hoping he'll understand. I consider asking him for a hit of acid, but I know that's just wishful thinking. If there's anything I shouldn't be doing right now, it's getting fucked up. Looking at Hayden sweating like a pig with pupils so big her eyes look like pits, I know that I won't be able to deal with this shit if I'm tripping. Katie, I now presume, is the one who sent the video and who killed the birds, stole the scissors, too. Definitely her MO. In fact, now that I'm thinking of her as a suspect, it doesn't seem so strange anymore. Murdering innocent animals so she can use their life force like macabre Crayolas? Right up Katie's

alley. Raped her whole life, tortured incessantly, starved. It's a wonder *she* hasn't killed anyone yet. If she does decide to go rogue though, I'm probably first on her list.

"I know, but I think you should."

"I'm not suicidal," I tell him as Hayden leans back and grabs his shirt in two fistfuls, glancing at me over her shoulder.

"You can't have them both, you know," she murmurs at me, and then goes back to trying to kiss Dax. He gently pushes her back and tries to help her lay down in bed; she lets him but then tries to spread her legs. She's not wearing underwear under that short skirt of hers. What a surprise.

"I'll deal with her," I tell him as she grabs at the fingerless glove on his hand and slides it off seductively. "But please, just go away."

Dax purses his lips and the pale skin on his face gets even paler. This is him getting angry. Doesn't happen often, but when it does …

"Why? Because you don't want to hear what I have to say? Because you don't want to know how I feel about you?"

I reach over and snatch Hayden's hands away from Dax, clamping her wrists together in my hand, cuffing her with tight, angry fingers. She giggles and struggles a bit, but it's all a show. She's not even trying. Anorexic bitch

can fight. Trust me, I've been on the receiving end of those blows. Do I hit back? Sure. Does it still hurt? Fuck yeah, it does.

"You mistake my actions for an emotional response," I hiss as I drag Hayden off the bunk closest to Dax and shove her into the bathroom. She's got that squinched up face on that says she's about to puke. A few seconds later, she does. Right into the bathroom sink. Hot dog. Much easier to clean up. "When in all reality, it's just indifference. Leave me alone, Dax, and keep your confessions to yourself." *God, Naomi. Harsh, much?* I know that the words I'm saying are a little intense, but I'm emotionally tapped out right now, and it doesn't look like I'm going to be let out of the ring anytime soon. I don't need Dax adding anything else to the mix.

"Oh? Huh. Seemed like you were more than willing to spill your heart out for Turner." I ignore Dax's words, refusing to get drawn into an argument. Why bother? What's the point? I sweep Hayden's hair away from her face, pulling back the pale hazelnut locks to keep them from getting covered in puke. The less mess I have to deal with, the happier I'll be. When she leans too far forward and smacks her forehead against the faucet, I can't hold back a smirk. "Fine. Don't talk to me. Ignore me." I hear rustling behind me and soon Dax's hand is coming up over my shoulder and flashing something in

my face. "But you might not want to ignore this."

The item clatters to the countertop next to Hayden and footsteps sound down the hall behind me. Before I pick it up, I stick a cigarette in my mouth and lift Hayden up by the shoulders, pulling her skirt up and pushing her down on the toilet. I leave her there to do whatever it is she needs to do and pause for just a second to pick up the small, round object. As I exit the bathroom, it takes me a second to register the sight.

The piece of plastic cupped in my palm has eyes and hair. It's a head. A doll's head. And inside of it, a business card with the address of the clinic in Tulsa.

The cigarette falls from my mouth and hits the floor, my stomach churns, and my hand clenches tight. When I open my fingers, there's nothing left but shattered bits of plastic.

CHAPTER 18
&TURNER CAMPBELL &

I'm so fucking pissed right now.

I get onstage and I scream my rage into the microphone; the crowd goes mad wild. Chicks throw their bras and panties at me; dudes start fighting in the mosh pit. Everything just goes crazy. My energy becomes their energy and soon the whole room is a roiling mess. When I'm done, I throw my mic to the floor and kick it offstage – the speakers screech and Milo intercepts me on my way out.

"Don't fuck with me," I tell him as I try to get ahold of my emotions, to understand them. I run my hand through my hair as sweat pours down my face, soaks my shirt, just fucking drenches me. I want to pace back and forth,

like a tiger in a cage. Behind me, the crowd is yelling for an encore. Fuck them. I'm trembling with rage, and I'm pretty sure that the next words that come out of my mouth aren't going to be so pretty. Best I don't screw up my career over some chick.

Naomi.

That's how I've got to fucking think about her, how I always should've thought about her. I don't know when things turned different. Because I thought we were connected somehow? I don't friggin' know. Whatever it was, it was a mistake, a momentary lapse in judgment. I let that itch under my skin turn into a raging fire that's ripping me apart from the inside out.

"Turner, I don't want you doing anything you might regret," Milo says, and I spin around, more than willing to take my frustration out on my manager. His pale blue eyes stare calmly back at me, but his hands are shaking and his tie is loose and crooked. He's scared. I don't know if he thinks I'm going to hit him, or if I'm going to storm out of here and make an ass out of myself. Whatever the reason though, he has a right to be afraid. I'm *this* close to exploding right now.

"What do you know about any of this?" I ask, getting up in Milo's face. He's shorter than me, blonde and pale, wispy. Not very intimidating. "Just do your fucking job and play damage control, got it? I own you, remember?

Want to keep your fucking job? Then clean up the shit I leave for you."

With that, I turn away and shove past Treyjan who's watching me with nervous eyes, out the doors, through the darkness.

One little secret has changed everything.

This is exactly why I hate them so much. Nothing good ever comes from keeping one. If Naomi had told me she was pregnant, I would've … *What, Turner? Married her? Swept her off her feet?* I spit at the floor. Fuck. I probably would've told her to do exactly what it was that she'd done.

I wish my brain wasn't so scrambled, and in that moment, I know I'll do anything to feel like myself. Coke will help. I know it will. A few bumps and I'll be me again – strong, prepared, ready for fucking anything. I've worked too hard to let something like this bring me down, and hell, why should it? Why should I give a shit at all? Fuck Naomi Knox.

I hit the bus and fly up the steps, storming into the back where we keep the good shit, stuffed into a locked drawer, so our fucking roadies don't skim off of us. As I'm digging around, pulling out an obscene amount of cocaine, in walks the woman of the hour, Miss Naomi fucking Knox.

I turn around with an eight ball in hand expecting to

see Jesse or Treyjan or Ronnie.

My heart starts to pump furiously at the sight of her and my cock gets rock hard. I squeeze the bag of cocaine so hard that I can feel the plastic bulging beneath my fingers, getting ready to burst open and spill white powder across the floor.

Naomi is standing there in her white button up and short skirt, eyes narrowed on me and hands shaking. We're no more than eight feet apart, and the air between us is red hot. My jeans feel tight, and my lower back is drenched with sweat. Fuck. Naomi is pretty, but I've been with lots of pretty girls. It's not just that, but I have no clue what the fuck it is. I take a tentative step forward.

"What do you want?" I ask her, and I can see her lip curling, can tell she wants to tell me to fuck off and leave her alone, but she's the one that came here, so I'm going to ask the questions. "And how the fuck did you get in here?" Naomi pauses in the doorway and the pin that's holding her shirt together comes loose, gaping open and flashing me the bra that was peeking out from beneath, giving me a nice, long, uninterrupted view of a smooth belly and the silver skull piercing that's stuck through her bellybutton.

"Your bouncer likes me better than you apparently," she says, and although I can tell she's trying to come

across as snarky and apathetic, it isn't working. There's a quaver there, like she isn't a hundred percent sure of herself. Naomi bites her lip hard and closes her eyes, shaking her head and taking a small step back. "I ... don't know why I even came here. I ... " Naomi lets her eyes flick open and cuts me into pieces with her stare.

I want nothing more than to charge through the space between us and grab her hard, possess her, change the looks she gives me from disgusted to admiring. But she's like a frightened kitty cat, standing there, ready to run away and never look back. I move carefully, ignoring the pain in my bandaged arm for the moment. If I think about it, I'll just get pissed again.

I walk forward, forcing myself to take my eyes from hers and focus on something else, something inanimate, something that won't judge me with every blink of its long, dark eyelashes. I grab my wallet from the drawer in the kitchen and sit down at the table, using my credit card to lay out four perfect lines – two for me and two for her.

"Sit," I tell her, noticing as I do that my hands are shaking already. *What the fuck?* I should've just gone out and found a nice girl from the audience to make me feel better. That would've taken my mind off things for sure. Maybe I'm so screwed up because I haven't fucked in days? Jesus. Since losing my virginity at age thirteen, this is the longest I've ever gone without sex. All this

holding out for Naomi is going to drive me nuts.

I pull a twenty from my wallet and roll it into a tube, leaning over the table and pressing one end to my nose, the other to the line of white on the granite surface below. Holding one nostril closed with my finger, I sniff up the bump and snort hard, absorbing the drug into my system while Naomi watches from the doorway.

"I didn't come here to do coke with you, Turner." Naomi pauses and tucks some hair behind her ear. Her eyes are conspicuously dry today, like a dust storm's just come through and coated them with a fine layer of dirt. I wonder what would happen if I wet them a little? After all, can't complain about a wet girl on my bus, not even if it's Naomi Knox. "I came here to warn you."

"Warn me?" I ask as I snort the other line and gather the rest of the powder together with my credit card, sniffing up the last remnants, making sure I get every last spec. "About what? You? You gonna come at me with a knife again?" *God, dude, you are a fucking dick.* I realize that, but I don't do a thing to change it. When I thought I had a kid, even for that brief period, I was going to. I had a reason. Now? Not really. Things were good before Naomi; they can be again. Sure, she's intriguing, but I can't let her consume me like this. I saw what obsession did to Ronnie, and he's fucked up good. I should feel blessed that there's no kid.

But I don't.

I just feel … empty.

I toss the twenty on the table and lean my head back against the cushions, waiting to feel like a superhero.

"I don't know how to say this without explaining everything," she says, and her voice sounds so tired that it makes me groggy. I raise my face up until I'm staring at her again and pat the leather bench next to my left thigh. If I don't have sex with this girl here, tonight, then I'm going to stay trapped. It's time to free myself, time to fuck her good and then forget all about her. I'm sure once I do, she'll blend into the endless line of faces and bodies in my memory, become nothing but a distant memory. *Bullshit.* I ignore myself and watch her closely.

Naomi's so shapely, got a body that won't quit. She's curvy with full tits that aren't saggy at all. They're plump and full and they don't even look like they need a damn bra to hold them up. Perfect chest to hip ratio, a tiny waist, long legs, smooth skin. She's like a fucking dream. Physically anyway. Mentally, she's a mess.

"If you're really going to cut that tat off, it'll be easier with a bit of help." I roll the twenty towards her. "And maybe you can slice mine off, too, huh? Give us both a clean slate." I'm joking, of course, but Naomi's moving forward softly, tentatively.

"I really did come here to warn you. There's this girl

… " I smile wickedly.

"There's always a girl."

"Fuck, Turner!" Naomi slams her palms down on the table and leans in close, so that when she yells, flecks of moisture tease my lips. "This is serious shit. I don't know how far she'll go or what she'll do. I don't even know if she gives a shit about you, but I had to come here." She pauses and sucks in a deep breath. I watch her chest rise and fall, focusing on the broken heart tattoo between her breasts. *I wonder if that has anything to do with me.* "Just one more mistake in a line of stupid decisions regarding you." She whispers this last bit under her breath and snatches up the twenty, scooting in next to me and snorting both lines in rapid succession.

For a few minutes, we sit quietly and stare at one another. The air is still hot and pulsing, begging us to close the distance between our bodies, to wrap around one another. God, if I could get ahold of her, we'd be fucking like rabbits.

When Ronnie and Treyjan climb the steps and find us there, Naomi jumps, acting like she's been bit.

"I gotta go," she says, standing up suddenly and pushing past them, so she can squeeze out the door before I even get the chance to yell after her. Stuffing a cigarette between my lips, I take off and chase her down before she even gets a hundred feet from the door.

"You gonna spill that shit and leave me hanging? Who the fuck are you talking about?" I light up and let Naomi lead me back to the venue. It's open all night long, so it's still rocking, jumping with a crowd about half the size it was when I was onstage but so fucked up that it feels ten times bigger. I smell another secret, a big one. Smoke trails after me as I keep close to Naomi's heels and slide in the back door behind her, moving past our roadies tangling with equipment and smoking joints, down the steps and into the crowd.

Thankfully, it's dark enough in here that nobody recognizes us, and we blend into the tattooed and pierced bodies, dressed in band tees and black, silhouetted against a dark wall drenched in stickers. The whole place smells like pot and booze and the music that's playing is grainy and barely audible over the screaming and shouting going on in here.

I fucking love it.

I don't love it so much when Naomi bursts into the girls' bathroom and leaves me hanging. I pause for a moment, glance around, and follow her in. The lighting in this shit hole is dim enough that I could get mistaken for a chick. Maybe. I smirk and lock the door behind me.

Neon lights flicker overhead from the crooked piece of plastic that hangs from the ceiling, swinging back and forth slightly with the air from the vent above the stalls. Graffiti and stickers cover most of the yellowing tile, and the rest is stained with God only knows what. I lean back against the door and keep smoking. The coke intoxication is starting to hit me now.

Naomi leans over one of the sinks and lets her blonde hair fall around her face like a curtain.

"Go away, Turner," she says, but there's no heat behind her words. Well, not anger anyway. I guess there's plenty of … something. Lust, I guess? I'm not sure. I stare at her, let my eyes glide down her body, from the firm set of her shoulders to her round ass, the leather boots that cover up the tattoo of my name. I flick my cigarette onto the floor and start to check the stalls, kicking in the doors as I move down the line. Naomi raises her head and watches me in the dirty mirror. Somebody drew devil horns there in red lipstick and they just happen to line up perfectly with Knox's head. How trippy is that? "What are you doing?"

"Oh come on, Naomi. You know what needs to happen just as well as I do."

"Um, actually, I have no fucking clue what you're talking about, so just spit it out for me and let me hear it." Naomi turns around and waits for me to finish. Good. There's nobody in here but us. Somebody knocks at the door and Naomi tells 'em to screw off.

My smile gets a little bigger.

"You know it; I know it. We gotta fuck, Naomi." She rolls her eyes at me.

"You're a real piece of work, you know that?" she asks, vehemence dripping from every syllable. I take a step forward and she stiffens. I pause and light another cigarette, watching as her eyes trace the lines of my lips as I slide it in nice and slow.

"And you're not? You come at me spouting some shit about a dangerous bitch on the loose and refuse to explain yourself. Are we talking about that skinny, anorexic chick? The one with the small tits."

"Jesus fuck," Naomi whispers, letting her eyes close for a moment. "Hayden Lee. You don't remember screwing her, do you?" I shrug and tap some ashes on the floor. Not a big deal; they join up with wads of toilet paper, gum, even a few dirty T-shirts. Interesting.

"Not really, no. She must not have been all that impressive then."

Naomi's face drops for a moment before she picks herself back up and starts towards the door. *Fuck. Wrong thing to say.* I chase after her, but when I grab her elbow, she pushes it back hard and hits me in the stomach. For a second, my anger gets the better of me, and I end up grabbing her rough, too rough maybe and spinning her around, slamming her wrists above her head.

When I kiss her, she bites me so hard that I bleed, but I don't stop, not even when she tries to knee me in the balls.

"Go to hell, Turner," she says, looking me in the face, tensing her muscles as she tries to get free from my grip. "Never again, I already told you that. You and me, not gonna happen."

"Doesn't have to," I whisper against her face, my breath heating her skin, making her squeeze her eyes tight. When they flicker open, they're full of rage. "Just once. That's all I'm asking. Then you and I can move on and forget the past, the tattoos, the abortion."

"Easy for you to say," she growls, and I can see it right there in her gaze. She fucking hates me. Loathes me. The emotion's so powerful that I almost step back, almost. But then I notice a twinkle hidden deep down in there. I think it's lust. I drop one hand between her legs and slide my fingers up her inner thigh. *Oh fuck yeah. It's hot and moist down there. Ready. She's ready for me.* An image surfaces in my mind briefly, a passing blur of color and heat, slickness wrapped around my cock. *Naomi.* I lick my lips. I have to have her again. I have to. There's no other option. "You're not the one that suffered."

I bend forward to kiss her again, and she breaks free, shoving me back so hard that I hit the stall door and

nearly fall into the toilet. When I right myself again, I see that Naomi's turned around and is in the process of unlocking the door. I move forward fast and slam her into the dented wood, sliding the zipper down on my pants, listening to the click of metal teeth.

"Tell me you're not interested," I whisper in her ear, noticing with pleasure that she shivers and squeezes her fists into two, tight little balls. "Tell me to stop and go away, and I will. I'll never bother you again." Risky gamble I'm taking here. If she tells me to leave, I don't know what I'll do. I'll be so obsessed with this chick that a thousand women, a thousand hits won't be able to cure me. This is my last chance to escape. *Or became enraptured forever.* Again, I ignore the side of myself that knows better. Old habits die hard, right?

"I hate you," she tells me, and I can hear in her voice that she means what she says. But she doesn't tell me to stop. I let my cock spring free and release her, using my hands to slide her skirt up her hips. Naomi's got on a nice, little thong leaving her ass bare and perfect, sexy and round. I tease her crack with my dick, watching as sweat beads on her skin and slides down her legs. I want to spin her around, so she can see me, watch me fucking her, but I'm afraid she'll run if I do.

"Do you have a condom?" she asks, voice muffled a bit, like she's afraid the sound will break the heat between us. Not going to happen. I feel like I'm drowning in a pool of molten lava. Every inch of me is on fire right now, sizzling, giving me an unbearable ache that has to be filled. *God, I'm horny as fuck.* I release her hips and grab her shirt, pulling it down her arms and tugging it off, tossing it into the sink next to us. Mine follows close behind, so I can press my skin against hers, grind us together into the dirty bathroom door. "Turner." Naomi's voice is no-nonsense right now, like I can tell she won't take any of my shit. Not that I blame her, but as I stand there and feel her body with my fingers, bits of memory start to come back to me, and I realize I *don't* want to use a condom.

Part of me wants to mess with her, tell her I put one on already, satisfy the desire that's grabbing hold so tight I can barely breathe. But I don't. For once, I think of someone other than myself. I don't realize it yet, but hey, there it is. I reach into my back pocket and pull out a condom. The package is custom with Indecency's logo on the front (Ronnie's idea, not mine): red with a white goat's head, black horns, X's over the eyes, tongue lolling.

Naomi starts to struggle, and I let her go, taking a step back, so she can get a full shot of me. I kick off my boots and push my jeans down, so I'm standing there butt friggin' naked. I like it better that way, seems more natural or whatever. Naomi faces me and locks my gaze

with hers, retrieving a pair of sunglasses from her pocket. She slides them up her nose and purses her lips. "Can I see it?"

"Sure." I hand it to her with a grin, knowing all the while that she's gotta be checking me out. Has to be. My ego won't let me think otherwise. "Best balloons in party city." I think she rolls her eyes, but I'm not sure. Fucking shades. Naomi spins the package every which way looking for what, I don't know, but when she's satisfied, she lifts her chin and reaches up to undo the front clasp of her bra. It falls to the floor along with her skirt, but she leaves her boots on. Clever girl.

"This is going to be quick, impersonal, and then it's going to be over? Is that understood?"

"Don't have to tell me twice," I say as Naomi wets her lips and steps forward, peeling open the condom package and removing the rubber. Lube glistens on her fingers as she switches it from her left to her right hand and curls her fingers around the base of my cock, obscuring the bat tattoos that wrap my shaft, caught in spiderwebs. Winged, but trapped. Desperate to be free, but doomed. I liked the symbolism, so I got it done – thankfully it's a tat I can actually remember getting.

The condom goes on quick and then Naomi steps back, leaving an entire foot of space between us. The air goes cold and then hot; music throbs like a dirty

heartbeat, shaking the walls and killing the lights.

CHAPTER 19

& NAOMI KNOX &

I see Turner standing there naked, abs tight and body slick with heat and sweat. His thick cock stands up proudly between his legs, just another piece of art added to that perfect body. He's so covered in tattoos that it's hard for me to take them all in: spiders, wolves, paw prints, bats, webs. He wets his lips, flashing me his tongue stud for just a moment before the light in the bathroom goes out with a spark.

A second later, our bodies crash together so hard it hurts, and I find myself on my back on the dirty, disgusting fucking floor, my hips cradled in Turner's hands, his cock pressing eagerly at my opening. It happens so fast, sliding in balls deep before I get a chance

to think this through, to protest.

I blame the cocaine.

The music continues to blast from outside the door, and I can hear people screaming, shouting, begging for more. It's loud but not loud enough to block the guttural groans clawing their way out of Turner's throat, blending in seamlessly with my rapid breathing, so that we're practically playing a song of our own. I want to think of it as a requiem, but somehow I imagine that it's a prelude.

Shit.

My hands curl, fingers clawing at the tiles, sliding through bits of soggy toilet paper and discarded tampon wrappers. I should be disgusted, but I'm not. I'm excited, thrilled even. All this time hating Turner, wishing him ill, wanting him dead, has built up into this angry sexual fervor that begs me to ride him until my heart explodes from my chest and my fingers draw blood from his back.

I drag my nails down his spine, wrap him so tight that our sweaty bodies slide over one another, mixing heat and warmth, skin against skin. His balls tease my ass, and his mouth drops to mine. I nibble his tongue ring harder than I probably should, hurting him with my teeth while he grinds his hips so hard into mine that I feel like we're both going to break, that our bones are going to shatter and leave us a messy, dirty puzzle on the floor.

We don't speak. Why bother? We have nothing to say

to each other with words that we can't say with our bodies right here, right now, rutting on the floor like a pair of wild cats, tails flicking, ears back, claws bared.

Turner breaks away from me and goes for my nipples, using his stud to flick them hard and bring chills over my body while goose bumps spring to life and betray me, letting him know how damn much I'm enjoying all this.

And I shouldn't be.

He fucked me over before, left me with that horrible decision …

But I still don't hate him as much as I should. Why? Why? Why?

I arch my back and press into him, drawing myself off the cold floor as much as I possibly can, letting Turner slide an arm beneath me, so he can prop me up. Like a phoenix rising from the ashes, I sit up and end up straddling Turner somehow, draping my arms over his neck and drawing his face back to mine.

And suddenly, the lights are flickering back to life, highlighting our faces with brightness and shadow both, making me see him, his expression, the desperation there that he doesn't even know he has. That passion he's carrying around, that intensity that he hides behind the arrogance and the fucking and the drugs, is showing and it's starting to stick to me. It was only a matter of time, really. I think I'm just hitting him at the right place, right time. *But you know that isn't entirely true. That first night, you two had a connection. You knew it; he knew it. He might've been fucked out of his mind, but he didn't get that tattoo because he was drunk. He got it because he liked you then, just like he does now. Turner doesn't want someone who'll roll over and take it. He wants someone who fights. He wants you.*

I call bullshit on my brain as Turner reaches up and grabs my glasses, throwing them so hard that they smash into the wall behind me and shatter into a million pieces. I grab his chin with my nails, pressing so tightly that little dots of red show up, highlighting his pale skin, the stubble on his jaw, that cocky smile.

"You're wet," he says, and I kiss him, just so he'll shut up. Doesn't close his eyes though. The bastard leaves those wide open and stares straight at me, does the one thing I don't want him to do and crawls inside, figuratively that is. My hips start to slow, pausing that ridiculous grinding motion I've been swinging, and Turner goes nuts.

With a growl, he grabs me and presses me down so hard it hurts, lets his head fall back, so I can bite and kiss the tattoos on his throat. I think of him onstage, how he can switch from his angel persona to his devil one, just like that, and my body squeezes tight, drags an orgasm screaming from his mouth at the same moment it pulls

one from mine. Like some fucking fairytale couple, we come together, and my heart stops and time stops, and then I'm up and stumbling away, grabbing my skirt, his T-shirt.

I throw the two pieces on, panting, sobbing even though I don't know why. When I grab the door handle and tear out of there, Turner is too slow to stop me.

I stumble back to the bus and climb on, shoving past Dax and Hayden, disappearing into my bunk and clamping my headphones around my ears, cutting out the world. I turn the music up so loud it hurts, makes my head spin in wild circles.

I can't.

I don't.

You cannot love someone you don't know, I remind myself, thinking back to our first time. I know *of* Turner. I've read articles about him, watched him onstage, listened to his music. That doesn't mean I know a damn thing about the real guy hidden underneath – other than that he's a complete and total asshole. A whore. A drug

addict. There's just nothing to like basically.

Still, I keep my headphones on and I rock back and forth to the music with the curtain closed and my eyes squeezed shut so tight that they hurt. I don't expect Turner to come after me since that was the deal we made, but somehow, I hope that he does. And I don't. And I do. I'm such a fucked up mess that I actually forget about Katie and Eric and the double homicide I committed. Pretty intense, huh?

Even Hayden leaves me alone for the rest of the night, and nobody complains about how loud the music is, even though I play it non-stop until we leave the next morning, pulling out of the parking lot and starting down the highway like nothing's different.

Everything is.

When I climb out of bed, I go straight for the shower and wash my skin so hard it hurts and turns a pale shade of red. I dress myself in Turner's tee (don't ask me why) and a pair of skinny jeans. I don't bother with undergarments, but I do slip on a nice, thick pair of boots, keeping that tattoo on my ankle as closed in as possible. I can't believe that I actually cut it. Now, it hurts so bad that I have no choice but to think about it. Constantly. Fucking Christ.

"What happened to you last night?" Hayden asks, staring straight back at me, all blue eyed and bushy tailed.

I want to punch her. Instead, I sit down and force myself
to eat the pancakes that America just whipped up. As she
starts in on her usual morning bitch session, I take a look
around the table. At least I'm not the only one that looks
miserable. Dax looks like he wants to shoot himself
between the eyes; Kash is green in the face; Blair has a
permanent frown sewn to her lips, and Wren is so hung
over, he can barely sit up.

Hayden scoots closer to me and scoops some hair
behind my ear, leaning over to breathe hot against my
skin.

"I need to talk to you in private," she tells me, licking
the side of my jaw. Blair watches her do this and makes a
What the fuck face? which I have no choice but to look
away from. If I don't let Hayden get away with little
teases like this, I can't fight her on the big ones. Like the
Turner thing. At the thought of his name, my pussy goes
into overdrive and my whole body feels sick. I'm both
horny and absolutely repulsed at the same time. With a
groan, I bury my face in my hands and then stand up.

Whatever it is that she wants, it's going to be bad. I
just know it.

Without asking questions, I follow Hayden into the
back and watch as she makes herself comfortable on my
bed, reaching into her pocket and drawing out a small
container. From inside, she picks out a hit of acid and

places it under her tongue.

I put my hands on my hips and watch her carefully, examining her from head to toe in case there's something I should be clueing in on. She's got on enough makeup that she looks like she's ready to start work over on second street, and the pink tank she's got on is see through enough that I can see her nipples. Classy.

"What?" I ask her. I'd like to get this over with before she starts tripping and ends up with hallucinations of demons trying to rape her. God, I hate it when this bitch is shit faced. She's a real train wreck, almost worse than when she's sober.

"I need you to do me a favor."

"No," I say automatically, although I already know that I'm going to do it. I touch a hand to my belly and refuse to think of Turner Campbell. "What?" Hayden sits up suddenly and her eyes shift from side to side like she's paranoid or something. Or maybe she took drugs I don't know about earlier in the morning. Who the fuck cares?

"Tomorrow night, you're going to sing for me," she says and my eyebrows shoot straight up to my hairline.

"What?" Hayden wanting to not only give up the spotlight entirely, but give it to me? What the fuck is going on here? "You're tripping hard. I'll come back later." I start to walk away, but she reaches out and wraps

her fingers around my wrist, reminding me of Turner's strong grip and the feeling of his hard body pressing against mine. My nipples harden instantly, and I tear myself away from Hayden.

"Do this for me, and I'll stop," she says, sitting up and then leaning over so that her head nearly touches the bed and the rumpled, black sheets. "I'll stop holding … that … over your head." She snaps her gaze up to mine, and her blue eyes are desperate, coated with a fine sheen of wetness. "America is going to flip out if she … " Hayden sits up suddenly and glances around me, but our manager is off composing a Tweet or some shit and isn't here to eavesdrop. Spencer's music from up front trickles back and gives us even more privacy. "I need you to keep her distracted until it's too late, until you get onstage. Just tell the crowd I'm on the rag or something." I wrinkle my nose at her.

"You've got to be fucking kidding me," I say to her, plating my hands on my hips, feeling bruises there, indents where Turner's fingers claimed me. I drop my hands to my sides. "I do this, and you stop ordering me around? Stop asking me to clean up your puke? That sort of thing?"

"You're home free," she whispers, and while I don't exactly like her tone, what can I say? This is too good to be true. I've been Hayden's bitch for *years* now. To be

free would be … I can't even express the emotion in words.

"How do I know you're telling the truth?" I ask her and watch as she rises to her feet, moves across the hall and digs under her pillow. When she reemerges, she's got a photo clutched in her hand. Hayden takes a deep breath and presses it to her boney chest. For a second there, she looks terrified, but I figure it's just the acid and don't worry about it. I wonder if I should.

"You've got my word, Naomi." Hayden searches my face for a long moment, pupils dilating rapidly, breath coming faster and faster. "You've been a good friend," she tells me, and I have to admit I'm stunned as shit to hear that. It's the first time she's said something nice to me since we graduated high school. Or rather, since *she* graduated high school. Me, I'm just a loser fucking dropout. "I know I haven't treated you right, and I'm sorry. I just wanted to keep you around, and I was afraid if I stopped teasing you, you'd go." I stare straight at her and don't say a word.

When she finally presents me with the photograph, when I look down at it and see the image that's burned to film, I throw up in my mouth a little.

"Oh, fuck."

CHAPTER 20
TURNER CAMPBELL

I am trashed as shit, but not from the coke, from Naomi Knox.

My head hangs over the sink and my hands curl with rage. At her, at myself, at whoever gets in my fucking way. I've already ripped Josh a new one today, and Milo … Well, let's just say that he's been avoiding me like the plague, hasn't knocked or bitched once, and I've been in the bathroom all night fucking long.

"Dude, some of us need to shower." It's Treyjan, of course. Nobody else has the balls to talk to me when I'm like this. I feel hungover from *Naomi*. She's in my blood now. And I thought I was going to be able to get her out of my system. A harsh laugh tears its way out of my

throat before I rip open the door and shove Trey back hard. Nothing against him, but when I get upset, I fight. It's a condition that was pounded into my blood from my useless mom and her boyfriends.

A scuffle breaks out between us and escalates. Blows are exchanged and Ronnie and Jesse end up getting involved, pulling us apart, arms still swinging. Sweat and blood are pouring down my face and into my eyes, but Treyjan looks okay. Stupid fuck. I shrug Jesse off and wipe the crimson copper from my mouth with the fabric of my T-shirt, letting it fall red and soggy back against my belly.

"What's your problem, man? Ever since you started obsessing about that fucking bitch from Amatory Riot, you turned into a completely different person. You've known the cunt for like a week and already, you're a mess. God, she's fucking hot dude, but she isn't worth it. Jesus Christ."

I stand stone still for a moment and then I'm flying at Trey again, hitting him so hard in the jaw that he ends up on his back on the floor. Jesse grabs one of my arms while Ronnie takes the other, and I end up pinned down in the captain's chair next to our driver, a pretty redhead with green eyes. I don't know her name, never bothered to learn it. She's been off limits since day one. There's this twinkle in her eyes that says she's in love. I usually

don't bother with girls like that.

My friends pull their hands back slowly, tentatively.

"You okay now?" Ronnie asks as sweat beads on his upper lip, and he starts to pant. He's a wreck again today, just miserable looking. Bags under his eyes, shaky hands, pale skin. Fucked up because of a girl that died more than ten years ago. A freak accident stole her life and his soul. My biggest fear's always been that I'd end up like Ronnie. I've never told him that, but it's true.

"Fine," I snap, watching as Jesse tucks his hands in his pockets and looks at me through a fall of dark hair. He's glaring at me, pissed the fuck off for starting shit when there wasn't any. Screw him. I turn to the window and slam my head into the glass, closing my eyes and trying to figure out how to get a grip on my anger.

My hands fumble around my pockets and come up with a cigarette. When I flick open my lighter, I open my eyes and watch the signs on the side of the highway roll by. At least we're moving. That way I know I can't get up and go after Naomi. *No secrets, right Turner? You've been fucking lying to yourself ever since you saw her asleep on that couch. You know. You remember. You like this chick. You did back then and you do now. You wanted that kid to exist, so you'd have an excuse to chase her. Get over yourself.*

I stand up quickly, take a drag on my cigarette and

wipe my sweaty palms off on the thighs of my jeans, the ones I got from the teen section, the ones made for chicks. And I look fucking perfect in them. Jesse and Ronnie watch me nervously; Josh glares; Treyjan sips a cup of water and glances at me out of the corner of his eye. Milo starts to speak, but I hold up a hand to keep him quiet.

I'm twenty-eight fucking years old; I know what I want and how to get it at this point in my life. And now I know I want Naomi Knox. It's that simple, that easy.

I pull my cigarette from my mouth and take a look around, meeting the eyes of my friends carefully, so they'll know how serious I am right now. First person to laugh gets punched.

"I'm in love." I don't say *I think* or that *I might be.* The first step to being successful in anything is knowing yourself. A lot of people don't get that. I don't need to think shit over or take Knox to dinner. That shit is all circumstantial. When you know, man, you just fucking know.

I put my cigarette back in my mouth.

The bus stays quiet. Ronnie's mouth turns up in a sad smile, but otherwise, everyone's expression is just blank.

"In love?" Treyjan asks, and I get the feeling that I might have to punch him again. Right in the nuts this time. "You're not in love with that girl. You just feel bad

because of that sob story she fed you the other day, all of that abortion crap."

"Nah, that has nothing to do with it." I put out my cig in a nearby ash tray, and I swear to fuck, I feel better than I have in years. Lighter. Like I could float away or some shit. I rub my hands down my sweaty face. "I just like her. She's a fighter. She's ... strong."

"She's a bitch," Treyjan says, and I smile.

"That, too." I sniff, trying to clear my nostrils of dried blood, and then shrug. "You don't have to understand it or agree with it. You just have to fuck off and let me do my thing, okay?"

"Like make an ass out of yourself onstage?" he asks, looking more and more pissed off by the second. I snap my fingers and point at his chest.

"Exactly." Treyjan rolls his eyes at me, and my phone buzzes in my back pocket. When I pull it out, I see there's a message from an unknown number, and my chest gets tight. Naomi, maybe? I open it up with a flick of my thumb.

"This is the stupidest fucking thing I've ever heard in my life. Turner, you've never even had a damn girlfriend. I've known you since we were kids, dude. You're not in love; you're just infatuated. Obsessed." He continues to bitch while Milo clears his throat and jumps in, giving some bullshit speech about love and life that nobody's

fucking listening to. Least of all me.

On my phone, there's a picture, and in it, Naomi. Covered head to toe in blood.

CHAPTER 21

❦ NAOMI KNOX ❦

I'll admit, I'm the first to think that Hayden's request is bizarre. Despite my heckling, she won't tell me what she's planning on doing, but I figure that I've got the rest of the day to keep prying.

The picture she gave me is folded up, burning a hole in my back pocket. Even the idea that it's there is making me sick, but I leave it, knowing that despite the random 180 she's just pulled, she can't be trusted. This photo, as fucked as it is, gives me complete freedom from her. I keep reminding myself of that as I struggle to forget about Turner. It's hard, especially since I've been listening to Indecency's albums on repeat for the last few hours. His voice is just ... out of this fucking world.

Every time he growls, I get flooded with heat and can't keep the memory of his groaning out of my head.

Fuck.

I wander back to the front of the bus and watch out the front window as we pull into another parking lot. Jesus, but I'm tired of sleeping on this damn thing. I want a real bed. And Kash snores. And now, Dax won't stop staring at me. Not even for a second. If he knows that Turner and I slept together, he doesn't let on, but he does keep dropping hints about the damn baby head, asking where it came from and whatnot.

I can't wait until this tour is over.

The parking brake hasn't even been set when Turner comes storming onto the bus and up the stairs. His face is red and his eyes are wide. He looks like shit.

"What the fuck are you doing here?" I snarl at him, but he's already grabbing my wrist and dragging me down the steps. His grip is rock solid and his intent is clear – to get me out of earshot. But why? As Turner yanks me across the cement and towards some shrubs at the edge of the lot, I see a champagne colored car idling near the exit. I don't know for sure, but I'm willing to hazard a guess that Eric's the one inside. Hmm.

Turner stops only when we're cloaked in shadows, hidden from the lights of the venue by a windowless stone wall. His fingers relax, and then his phone's in my

face.

"Naomi," he says as I snatch it away from him, examining his wide eyes and sallow skin. I don't know what he's been doing all night, but sleeping certainly isn't it. And he's wearing the same pants he had on yesterday. Different shirt though. Probably since I ended up stealing his. I tap my fingers on the side of the phone and wonder what happened to my underwear. If they end up on eBay, I swear to God, I'll kill him.

"What is your fucking problem?" I ask him, switching my gaze to the screen and the picture that's already pulled up and ready for my viewing pleasure. My heart starts to pump and dizziness sweeps over me, making me stumble. Turner catches me, and out of the corner of my eye, I see Dax watching us. I keep the phone tucked tight against my chest. "Where did you get this?" I sound breathless, desperate. Afraid. And I don't like to sound that way. It isn't in my nature.

I look down again, examine the picture.

There I am with the scissors in my hand, pale fingers clenched tight around the metal. In this particular still, the pointed blades are half buried in Mrs. Rhineback's miserable throat. Blood is just starting to spill from her neck to join her husband's. Oh, how fun.

"A video followed shortly thereafter," Turner says, lighting up a joint. I steal it from him before he has a chance to smoke it and purse my lips around it. Wow. Just wow. Thanks a lot, Katie. I look up and let my eyes scan the darkness around us. She could be anywhere and that scares the shit out of me. She was never dangerous before, but people change. I have no idea what she's capable of. I mean, that baby head thing? That was just cruel.

My breath is coming in short, sharp gasps and my chest feels so tight that I'm afraid my ribs might just open up and let out my heart. As I drop Turner's phone to the ground, I notice that the lower half of his shirt is covered in blood. His swollen lip and nose explain the source but not the cause. I smash the heel of my boot into the screen and pull the joint from my mouth with one hand, gesturing casually, as if Turner didn't just discover the fact that I'm a murderer – one who got away with it.

"What happened to you?" I ask, noticing that my voice is still strained and weak. I'm not fooling anybody. I crush the phone into a pulp and Turner doesn't stop me. Instead, he steals his joint back and smokes it.

"Doesn't matter," he says, and I notice that his voice is just as weak as mine, so light that it nearly gets stolen away by a gust of dry wind that sweeps in and tangles my hair around my face. "The question is, what the fuck happened to you?" I look up at his eyes and notice that they're not judgmental. Nervous, maybe, but that's about

it. And he hasn't called the cops. At least I don't think so. They're not here now anyway.

"Who sent this?" I ask, realizing too late that I just destroyed any chance I might've had of tracking the message.

"Blocked number," he replies, shaking his head. "Which is fucking weird because there are, like, five people on this fucking earth that know mine." He takes another drag and hands the joint back to me. I stare at the strong lines of his face, the perfect jaw, the sloe-eyed gaze. Turner is one of those people that was born to be famous. He just oozes confidence, a natural born leader. I wonder when he's going to get it together and focus all of that intensity and that passion on one woman. God help her when that happens. Once he locks on, I doubt he'll ever let go.

"You tell anybody?" Turner laughs and then leans forward, putting his arm out and pressing his palm against the wall. I take a small step back, so we're not so close. I can still feel his sweaty body against me, still feel his hips grinding against mine. I look him in the face, meet his eyes unflinching. I just got free of Hayden, no way I'm going to become anybody else's bitch, especially not Turner's.

"You really had to ask?" he says and then he just stops, lets go, steps back. He puts his hands on his hips

and shakes his head. "God, I knew I smelled another secret. You got anymore I should know about?" I watch him carefully, trying to judge his mood, his intent. What's he going to do with this new information? How is he going to abuse it?

"That's the last one," I admit, trying to be as honest as possible. He nods like he believes me and rubs his hand over his stubbly jaw. His dark hair is mussy and unkempt, tangled and just a tad greasy. He's not so perfect right now, not his usual decorated self. And it's turning me on. Even through all of this shit, my pussy starts to pulse and I get soaked.

I bend down and start to scoop the bits of phone into my palm. No way I'm leaving them here for somebody to find. Even broken, they could still have information I don't want getting out. I'll burn them or something later.

"So what happened?" he asks again, bending down to help me, taking the joint back and trying to smirk at me. It falls flat. Turner's inked up fingers come out and brush against mine accidentally, sending chills down my spine.

"Well, to make a long story short," I begin, wondering when the demands are going to start trickling in. I wonder if he'll ask me to fuck him to buy his silence. I'm not a whore, so that'll never fucking happen. I try to come up with something I can offer, something that won't put me in the same position as I was with Hayden, where

she had the upper hand always. "I ... " Turner interrupts me.

"No, I don't want the abridged version." I hold open my palm and he drops the cracked bits of plastic into it. "Tell me everything." I roll my eyes as we stand up together, surreptitiously checking for any signs of Katie. She could just pop out at any moment and fuck me hard. Not that she isn't trying her best from afar. That is, if it's even her. I just kind of assumed it was, but you never know.

"Why?" I snap, forgetting for just a second that he has my freedom in his hands right now. I look down at the long fingers, at the cluster of stars, the paw prints. Doubt there's any rhyme or reason to the designs. After all, he'd fucking *forgotten* about my name on his back. I start back across the parking lot, but Turner grabs me around the arm and pieces of phone fly everywhere as he spins me in a tight circle and pulls me into his arms.

His hands dig into my back, rumpling my shirt, squeezing me hard, and his lips find mine, pressing, tongue sliding deep into me while his stud teases the sensitive flesh on the roof of my mouth. My entire body explodes into a million parts, comes back together and lights up the night sky with lust. I kiss him back fiercely, wildly, grabbing Turner's hair and tugging so hard that he groans into my mouth.

And then I shove him back violently, stumbling and falling to my knees as I scramble to recover as much of the phone as possible.

"What the hell was that for?" I growl at him, feeling strange. I can't put my finger on it, but something isn't right. I can't tell yet whether that's a good or a bad thing. Turner doesn't bend down to help me this time, but I can feel his eyes boring into my back. "If you think you can control me now … " Turner laughs at me, and the sound isn't entirely unpleasant.

"Oh, please," he tells me, smoking his joint and watching as I stand up and glare at him. He seems a lot calmer now, a lot less nervous. I realize then that I do, too. Much better. I look away and focus on the car near the exit. It's still there, waiting. I wonder if I should go over there. "Is that even a possibility?"

"So what do you want? Obviously, I need you to keep your mouth shut about this." I squeeze the broken pieces so hard that I draw blood into my palm, turning my gaze back to Turner again.

"Let me lay it out for you," he begins, running his fingers through his hair and cringing like he can't believe how dirty it is. "I won't tell your secret if you don't, how's that?" I stare at him like he's crazy.

"Come again?" Turner steps forward, and I step back. Car lights flicker across his face, and when I turn, the car

is pulling away. Strange. Turner grabs my chin and forces my gaze back to his. I come *this* close to punching him in the jaw again.

"I won't tell anybody what I saw," he says and then pauses like he's just thought of something. My throat gets tight. "But I want you to do one thing for me." My lip curls in disgust. If he asks me to suck his cock … "Forget that promise we made." I blink rapidly, confused.

"Promise?" Turner releases my chin and brushes some hair off my forehead.

"About being done with each other, not seeing each other. I changed my mind about that."

"I see." He grins and drops his hand, looking for all the world like a fucking devil again.

"And I want your story, all of it. From birth to death, or at least as close to it as you can get." He pauses again and rubs at his split lip with the back of his hand. "And I need to know all about *that* night, everything we did, everything I said."

"You're fucking nuts," I tell him, but I know I'll do it. I tell myself that it's just so he'll keep his big, fat mouth shut, but in actuality I'm just keeping another secret from myself.

CHAPTER 22
TURNER CAMPBELL

Naomi Knox is a murderer.

The thought doesn't bother me as much as it should. I get the feeling that the people in the video had it coming and try not to delve too deep into that line of thinking. She'll tell me about it. I can tell from her body language that she's already accepted that she has to spill her guts for me. If I find out they molested her though, I might go ballistic. Any man that thinks he can take a woman without her will disgusts me. Pathetic.

I trail behind Naomi and finish my joint, ending up standing in awkward silence next to her drummer friend while he glares at me, and she stashes the phone bits

somewhere in the back of the bus. I do my best to ignore him, pretty fucking sure that if something starts between us, it's gonna end up ugly.

I take deep breaths to calm my nerves and try to bring myself down from the nervous high I've been on all night. That video seriously screwed with my head. I mean, I admit to myself how I feel about this chick and then I get railroaded with crap like that? What a load of bull. Whoever sent it had some pretty fucked up intentions in mind. I point at the fridge and keep my eyes off that emo dude's face and on Naomi's ass as she bends down and messes with something under her bunk.

"I'm gonna grab a beer." I reach for the fridge door and yank it open, grabbing a couple cans and tossing one to Knox when she starts back this way. She catches it in her hand and then drops it in her purse, pausing next to me to reopen the fridge. She grabs a six pack and then gestures at me to follow her outside again, past groups of loitering people, trailers, buses, until we end up sitting on the curb as far from the action as humanly possible.

Behind us, the highway flashes with lights and rumbling engines, busy and getting busier. In the distance, I can see the sun rising up from behind the mountains. I pop the top on my can and swig it.

"I'm going to be blunt with you, okay?" she says, and I shrug.

"Haven't seen you as anything but," I tell her as I study her face and wonder when she'll figure out that I'm after her, for keeps this time. A smirk curls my lip, but I force it back. I can't let her know that I've come to this abrupt decision. She'll think I'm fucking nuts. *I* think I'm fucking nuts. Everybody does. But shit, when the heart wants something, it'll do anything to get it, and right now, mine's in a fucking frenzy.

"Well, I was born, put up for adoption, adopted." She puts her beer to her lips, and I watch as her throat works, swallowing the alcohol down like it's water. When she's finished, she takes a deep breath and crumples the can, tossing it into her purse and starting in on a second. I rush to catch up. Turner Campbell doesn't get drunk under the table. Nuh uh. "My adoptive parents were killed in a car accident when I was seven." She smiles tightly at me. "Am I going too fast for you?" I lick my lips and lean in close.

"You go as fast as you want, baby." My fingers trace down her upper arm, and she shivers. "But when you're finished, I might have you go back for all the little details." I smile, and Naomi curls her lip at me. She acts like we never fucked, and it annoys the shit out of me. I wonder if she's doing it on purpose. She can't lie to me though. No matter how she acts, what she says, what she does, I saw her eyes wet. Thinking back, I figure she

probably thought I meant something else. But all that dryness there was lit up for a brief second. I do my best to keep the smirk off my face.

"I want to know why you give a shit all of a sudden, why you care to know all those little details. What do you want from me, Turner?" I lean back with a sigh and put my arms out behind me.

"Okay, so they died and then what?" I ignore her question.

"Then I'm no different from every other troubled foster brat. I was bounced from place to place, ended up with a family who liked to fuck their own daughter, starve her, and beat her unconscious. When they came for me, I got rid of them. And then I went searching for you, found you, and left with an even bigger problem. I got an abortion and then I moved around the country for awhile." Naomi pauses and shakes her head hard, like she just wants to forget everything that ever happened to her. "I ended up back in Tulsa which was either a curse or a blessing, haven't decided which yet." She stops again to narrow her eyes. "Hayden and I formed Amatory Riot and then I ended up here. Any questions?"

I just sit there for a moment trying to process. Jesus Christ. Not exactly what I was expecting. I open my mouth several times and end up snapping it shut without saying a thing. What is there to say to that really? So I

fall back on what I'm comfortable with. Flirting. I run my fingers through my hair which is disgusting as shit. First thing I'm doing when I'm done here is taking a shower.

"Tons, but first, I want to know something else." Naomi sets her beer down and digs out a smoke, holding it delicately between two fingers as she stares off into the distance with clouded eyes. I watch her for a moment and then I look around, checking to see if there's anybody watching. We're pretty well hidden here, drenched in shadow surrounded by brightness, lost in plain sight. I do my best to hold back a grin. I can imagine all sorts of things we could get away with over here. Doubt Naomi would be up to any of it though. "What did we do that night?"

"Pardon?" she asks, blowing smoke out in rings. My cock goes stiff immediately. Smoke rings are kind of a fetish of mine. "You mean sexually?"

"What else is there?" I ask which garners me a sour look. She still doesn't respect me, fine. I can wait for that, but at least I'm not getting angry anymore. As soon as I admitted to myself that I was interested in Naomi, that stopped right away. I try to think of that as a sign that I'm not fucking around here. This is real life shit. "Yeah, sexually."

"Why?"

"Because I'm not telling the cops you stabbed your parents with scissors." Naomi jabs the cherry of her cig against the cement so hard that her fingers come back bloody, scraped raw by the rocky surface.

"Turner, listen to me right now. If you can't remember what happened that night, that's your problem. I'm not going to sit here and relive it with you. Look, I gave you my life story. That should be enough." I raise my brows at her and feel another stir of heat in my stomach. Okay, so maybe the anger didn't stop completely, but it's better. Anybody else talking to me like that … Let's just say, it wouldn't be good.

"You gave me a ten second rundown, that hardly qualifies." With a snarl she stands up and spins around to face me, taking her purse with her, getting ready to run away again. Fucking me didn't change her opinion of my character, I guess. Or she wasn't impressed. I look up at her and lick my lips. If I'm going to win this girl, I'm going to have to use a different approach. The Turner Campbell style is better equipped to rounding up groupies. I stay quiet.

"Turner, listen up. That girl I warned you about before is my foster sister, Eric's sister. She's the one that sent you the video." She pauses and chews the inside of her cheek. She's already backing up, getting ready to leave. "The reason I warned you about her is because she

might be dangerous. She's … fuck, how do I put this? She's obsessed with me." Naomi pauses and looks me straight in the face. "To the point where she was hospitalized for it. Now she's following me and she's doing … strange things. I'm going to say this once, so I hope you'll hear me out: be careful."

"You serious?" I ask her, but I can already tell from her facial expression that she is.

"Watch your back, Turner," she tells me as she turns away. "See you onstage."

I hop to my feet, ready to follow after her and then force myself to stay back. I've gotta get mentally prepared for this falling in love crap. This shit's a lot harder than I first thought. Besides, the war of love can't be won with greasy hair and sweaty fucking pits.

I head back to the bus to rethink my game plan.

CHAPTER 23
❦ NAOMI KNOX ❦

I storm across the parking lot, angrier than I was before, so pissed off that I can hardly think straight. My hands are shaking, and I see red. The problem is, I can't figure out why. Nothing happened just now, and I hardly told Turner anything. I was going to, was going to break it down, feed him every last detail, but then I remembered: I hate him. I hate him, and I fucked him yesterday. Gonna have to get used to dealing with that.

Dax tries to intercept me as I climb on the bus, but I ignore him. I could never love Dax because I ... because I hate Turner so much. There's not room for any other emotion inside of me right now. I thought I was okay, that I could fuck him and forget about all of it, but I'm

not. If I thought telling Turner about the abortion would free me from his hold, then the only person I was fooling was myself.

There's so much shit going on around me that I can barely breathe. I want to be empty and carefree and emotionless and instead, I get all of this drama and angst. Fuck.

I strip off my clothes in the middle of the hallway and don't care that Wren is probably whacking it to my naked body. I put on some underwear and a tank top before I fall into bed, forgetting until the last second that Hayden gave me that horrible photograph. Scrambling out of the sheets, I dig my pants out of the dirty laundry and try not to imagine what Spencer would've thought if she'd found it.

I unfold the image and stand looking at it, highlighted by a shaft of brightness that's leaking from the partially closed pocket door that separates the kitchen from the bunks.

I see Hayden naked, standing over a lifeless body. It's naked too, but it's hard to tell whether it was a man or a woman since it's soaked in red, beaten to a near pulp. Bile rises into my throat, and I crumple the image up in my hand, tucking it under my mattress for safe keeping. Hayden didn't tell me shit about this, and I didn't ask. What right do I have anyway? I've killed before, and my

guess is, so has she. The picture is just so fucking horrible that I don't even want to think about it. I don't want to know. Whatever it is, it's her secret to keep. All it is to me is a key, so it doesn't change anything. You know what they say – let sleeping dogs lie.

So I crawl into bed and slip my headphones over my ears. They're big fat ones, neon green, and they block out everything around me, sliding over my ears like shields. I turn the music up so loud that Wren actually comes over, jerks the curtain back and turns it down for me.

"You're not Beethoven, dude," he says, looking like a shadow creature in the dimness back here. I can't even see his face. "If you go deaf, you can't write us anymore music."

"Fuck you, Wren," I tell him and then turn over, doing my best to force my mind away from everything – Katie, Eric, Hayden … Turner. Turner. Turner. If I didn't know any better, I'd say I was obsessed with the man. After awhile, I give up trying to deal with this on my own and go for the pills I have stashed in the drawer beneath my bunk. I know just the right combination to knock myself out and make me forget, at least for a few hours anyway.

Once I've got a good night's (or day's I guess since the sun is rising outside the bus) sleep cradled in my hand, I down the pills and fall into the pillow. A short while later, Turner's face appears floating above me.

I'm so drugged up that I'm not sure if what I'm seeing is a dream or a hallucination or if Turner's really right there, bending down low, smelling like soap and mint toothpaste. He climbs into the bunk and slides the curtain closed, pulling my headphones off my ears but leaving the music on, setting them beside my head as he runs a hand down the side of my face.

I try to pinch myself, try to wake up, but I can't really move.

"I was thinking," he tells me, and I figure then and there that this must be a dream because there is no way in shit that Dax or America would let him come back here like this. They know how I feel about the stupid fuck, probably better than I do. "That you might be, like, my saving grace or something." Turner pauses and adjusts himself, curling forward so that he can sit in the tiny space of the bunk without any limbs hanging over the side. "I didn't know I even needed one, but that's the point, isn't it? Help comes along when you least expect it."

"Go away," I groan, batting at the air in front of me. Turner just smiles and stays right where he is. "I need to get some sleep or I'm never going to survive this shit." He adjusts himself, tucking his feet underneath his body, so he can lean over me and brush hair away from my forehead. I reach my hands up to push him off, certain that if I do, the dream will break and he'll go away. Instead, I come up against warm flesh and my fingers curl involuntarily, wrapping around his strong biceps.

"Tell me again, and I'll go," he says, smirking all the while, pressing a kiss to the pulse on the side of my throat. My heart flutters and my arms drop to my sides. I'm getting the most horrible déjà vu right now. I'm getting pulled back to that night when Turner Campbell punched a guy out for me and drove me into town, took me places, romanced the ever living shit out of me. The memory of getting tattooed flies past and then I'm sixteen again, lying on a bed in a hotel while Turner kisses and caresses every single part of my body, treating me like a goddess, promising me that I'll never have to suffer again, that he'll take care of me. Yeah, I knew he was fucked up then. Sure, I did, but I was so lonely and desperate that I wanted to believe him. I had nobody and nothing, and my soul was drenched in the blood of my foster parents, so what else was I supposed to do? My idol was promising me the world. It seemed to good to be true. I

should've known better.

So now, Turner, who I guess maybe really is there, is touching me, sliding my tank top up and over my head, running his fingers down my body, caressing my hips. I'm not sure what to do, trapped somewhere between that handful of pills and those memories. That's what I tell myself anyway. I refuse to admit that I actually want him there. That would be sacrilegious at best.

"Turner," I begin, but he stops me with a gentle kiss, one that's the complete opposite of the bloody teeth smashing thing we've been doing lately. He presses his lips tight against mine and runs his fingers down my body, pushing my legs gently apart. I think he's there to fuck me at first, but then he starts to tease the skin on my inner thighs, brushing his hand down to my knee and back up again, like he's petting a fucking pussy cat or some shit. But it feels so damn good that I let him, relaxing my head into the pillow and letting him massage my tongue with his.

After a few moments of this, Turner takes off my panties and then his shirt, laying across me so that my naked body presses against his skin and my bare crotch lines up with his clothed one. He's erect and ready, but he doesn't take off the sweatpants he's got on. Instead, he continues to touch and feel me, rubbing my breasts in gentle motions, gliding his palm across my nipples. His

actions are so unexpected, so unlike anything I'd ever think Turner Campbell would want to do that I convince myself once again that this is all a dream and try to relax into it.

Seriously, I've never had anyone but him touch me like this. It's intoxicating. I mean, it's not like I'm a virgin or anything, but let's just be honest, my sexual experiences have been limited to quick ruts and one night stands. The only boyfriend I've ever had was my damn foster brother and that never went anywhere at all.

"Why are you doing this to me?" I ask when it's clear that Turner didn't come here for sex. As mind boggling as it seems, I'm pretty sure he came here to prove that's exactly what he *wasn't* looking for. Or maybe he remembers that night, the way he skimmed my body with his lips, the way he teased my nipples with his tongue. Either way, I'm a bit shocked. Or I will be when these damn pills wear off. Right now, I just feel weightless, like I'm floating on a sea of feathers. Fuck.

"Why not?" he asks, and when he lifts his head and smiles at me, I know I'm in trouble. "You're enjoying this, aren't you?" And then Turner descends and buries his head between my thighs, cupping me under the ass with his hands and holding tight, locking me down and flicking his stud across my clit. Tears spring to my eyes and my back arches off the bunk, fighting against the

tight grip that Turner's got on me. *Holy shit, that feels fucking sickening.* Nice to know that mouth's good for something other than singing. And I'd thought that was his only talent. Silly me.

My fingers curl into the sheets as he works his mouth against my cunt, tasting me, not afraid to dive in and use his entire tongue to reach out and penetrate me, draw me into him. He leaves no spot untouched, gliding up and down with his lips, breathing against me, spreading me open and eating me out like he knows everything about me, like we've been together for years. It's fucking weird. Weird because I don't know him, weirder because he doesn't know me, weirdest because that's Turner fucking Campbell down there.

Just when I think he's about to finish and pull away, he slides his fingers into me, and I can't hold back. My body squeezes around him tight and my hands reach down to tangle in his hair. I pull his mouth up to mine and grind my hips against him while he teases me, sliding in and out, drawing gasping breaths that escape my lips and crash into his. All the while, I can feel his erection straining against his pants, begging to fuck me.

"Do it," I whisper, and he grins like he knows exactly what I'm talking about.

"Not tonight," he tells me, voice low and rough, like he's about to come in his pants. Still, that self-assured

look never leaves his face, and I just know, even through the haze of fatigue and pills and pleasure, that I'm never going to be able to live this down if I come in his fucking arms with tears rolling down my goddamn face. So I reach up and wipe away the moisture with my knuckles, and then before he can stop me, I'm thrusting my hand down his pants and grabbing his dick so tight that my nails cut into his skin and he bites my lip hard enough that I bleed. Seconds later he's blowing a fucking wad into his sweatpants and slamming his knuckles against my pussy, bruising my pelvic bone and drawing an orgasm out of freaking nowhere.

The pleasure grips my body like a vice and sends shockwaves rolling through me, leaving me a panting, shaking mess.

Turner withdraws his hand and wipes it on my blanket.

"God, Knox," he says as my eyelids start to flicker closed and the word spins around me. "You sure are something else, you fucking know that?"

Consciousness fades, and I pass out.

CHAPTER 24
TURNER CAMPBELL

As I'm leaving the bus, I run into that drummer dude again, the one with the ghosts on his arms. At first, I think he's going to move away and let me pass like he did that first night we met, but he doesn't. He actually blocks me at the door, stepping in front of me with his eyes narrowed and his lips pursed so tight that it looks like all the blood's been drained out of his face.

"Why her?" he asks me, gray eyes searching mine for an honest answer. Luckily for him, that's my policy anyway. Plus, I'm in a pretty good fucking mood. I just smirk when his gaze catches on the wet stain on my pants. I wear it like a badge of pride.

I rub my chin for a moment and try to figure out how

to phrase this while my head is swimming with bursts of images – an elevator, Naomi's upturned face, a bathtub. It's not much yet, not enough to actually put together anything solid, but the more time I spend with her, the more I remember our first night together. It's kind of shocking actually that anything at all has come back to me. Normally, when I lose a memory, it's gone for good. Not this one apparently. Instead of responding with words, I turn around and show him my bare back. I don't even have to say anything; he sees it.

"Fuck," he whispers, but he doesn't sound defeated, just annoyed. I turn back to face this dude, the one who has such a massive fucking hard-on for Naomi that it's practically blocking me from the door all on its own.

"What's your name again?" I ask him, trying to keep my tone low. Sure, I'm a little pissed off at this guy, but that just means I have to be more direct, fight harder. Anyway, I'm not worried, I've never lost a girl to another guy before. Somewhere in the back of mind, I know that isn't going to be the problem. The problem is going to be Naomi. She still hates me.

"Dax." Just the first name again. Guess he doesn't want this to get too personal. Too bad it already is. I take a deep breath and glance down at my bare feet.

"Well, Dax," I begin, knowing without knowing that whatever I did tonight was a step in the right direction.

"Naomi Knox isn't like any other woman I've ever met." I shrug because I'm not going to spill my heart out to this guy, not a chance. And anyway, I need to get out of here quick before Naomi wakes up and comes out to find me with my hands shaking and my skin flushed. If she finds out how much I just enjoyed that, she'll gain the upper hand. Yeah, I have to let her know how I feel, but I don't want her to just find out; I have to say it in my own words, on my own time. If that makes any sense.

"No, she's not," he confirms, swallowing hard and letting his eyes flutter closed. He's got words tattooed on the backs of his eyelids, but they're hard to read in the dim morning light. When he opens them, he looks at me with a challenge in his eyes. "And once she realizes that you're bad news, she'll move on, and I'll be here. I'm not giving up. I haven't even started yet." I smile back at Dax and I know that my face is getting a real wicked look on it right now. I'm not worried. Maybe I should be, but I'm not.

"You challenging me to a duel? Should we lock horns like a bunch of horny deer?" Dax stares at me, stoic and silent. "Alright then," I say, holding out my hand, knowing somehow that this is all for shit. Naomi's the one who will decide everything. But whatever, we're men and we're both pumped full of enough testosterone to fuel a small airplane. "You're on."

Dax shakes my hand, and I leave the bus promising myself that I don't feel any less confident. I wonder if that's true.

I can hardly sleep when I get back to the bus. I end up tossing and turning so damn much that Treyjan actually climbs out of bed, grabs me by the shoulder and rolls me onto the floor. I hit the ground with a grunt and come up ready to fight. Luckily, Ronnie's still awake and able to step in, separating us before anything bad actually happens.

As soon as he does, Trey crawls back in bed, tossing a glare over his bare shoulder at me, and Ronnie and I end up at the table with Josh and three cups of coffee. I'd rather not be sitting here with the little blonde fuck, but that's just the way it is, I guess. He stares at me with an accusatory gaze for so long that I end up chucking a small creamer at his face. It explodes on impact and makes him look like he just got jizzed on.

"What the fuck is your problem with me?" he shouts, standing up and nearly spilling all the coffee. I ignore him and lean back. Yeah, I'd like to beat the shit out of him, but I'm kind of still riding that Naomi high. She's good for me, I think. Again, Ronnie steps in and cools the anger simmering in the air. I mean, for a drugged up whore, he actually gives good advice and says some pretty wise shit. I think it comes from fucking up so much. He knows exactly when to stop, how much is too much, how little is too little, that sort of thing.

"Sit down, Josh," he says as I smirk and bring the coffee to my lips, clinking the mug against the piercings on either side of my lip. "Wipe yourself off and relax."

"Look, I'm tired of being shit on because I made out with the girl he likes. It's getting old. Besides, she fucking came onto me." My lips purse and my free hand curls against my thigh, but I keep the anger back. And I am so fucking proud of myself for that. "Besides, he doesn't deserve her anyway."

"Alright, that's fucking it." Ronnie reaches out a hand and stops me as I rise to my feet. There's a limit to everything, especially my newfound patience. Apparently, Josh wants to see just how far he can push me before I snap. "I'm tired of listening to this shit." Ronnie faces me and waits until I'm fully seated before he speaks again. When he does, he sounds tired and worn out, like he could go at any minute. The thought makes me sick to my stomach. I don't want to lose another

friend. As if he can sense what I'm thinking, Ronnie brings up Travis.

"He's not here to replace him you know."

"Bullshit." Ronnie smiles sadly.

"He's not. Nobody will ever replace Travis." I roll my eyes and try to keep calm, drumming my fingers along the back of the bench.

"Don't start spewing that love all, peace to the masses bullshit, Ronnie." Josh looks between him and me, face set in a frown. "Travis played bass; Josh plays bass. He's a replacement." *A shitty one.* I keep that last bit to myself and get out a smoke. I don't know why I'm trying to sit here arguing loss with Ronnie. He knows more about it than anybody.

"Turner," he begins, taking the lit cigarette from my hand and forcing me to go back for another. "Can I give you a little bit of advice?" I shrug.

"Sure, why the fuck not."

"Be careful," he begins, putting out the cig even though he hasn't smoked it yet. He's getting distracted and his eyes are starting to gloss over with memories. In a few minutes, he'll retreat to the bathroom to shoot up some meth. "With Naomi, I mean. Take this shit seriously, okay? Because once you fall in love, really fall in love, so deep that you feel like you're fucking drowning in it, you'll never be able to find a replacement.

Travis was our best friend, and he always will be. Bass or not, he was there in a way that nobody else will ever fill. It's the same thing with love – once she holds that spot, you'll never be able to get it back." He leans in close to me, and I notice then that his hands are shaking. "Do you understand me?"

"You sound like a fucking fag," I tell him, but his words make my stomach hurt and my head spin. I know they're true, and they scare the shit out of me.

A knock on the door startles us all out of the conversation, and I'm the first one up, padding across the floor and clicking the lock on the handle. Outside, it's just starting to get dusky, fading from day to night. Our useless fucking bodyguard is missing, but there's a box. I move down the stairs to pick it up and bring it back inside. There's no name on the package which kind of freaks me out. Normally, I'd throw shit like this away. Today, I'm feeling ballsy.

"What's that?" Ronnie asks, getting up from the table to come stand behind me. I shrug as I grab a knife from one of the drawers and slide it under the tape.

"Probably some naked pictures and a few used pairs of panties," I say with a grin. We've had worse delivered. I unfold the flaps and the grin dies right where it began, melting down my face with a spark of fear and a jolt of rage. Inside the box is Travis Gaborone's baseball cap.

CHAPTER 25

❧ NAOMI KNOX ❧

When I wake up the next morning, I feel like shit.

"Stupid fucking pills," I snarl as I struggle to sit up and run my hands down my face. Cold air hits my tits, and I realize suddenly that I'm naked and that my headphones are still sitting on my pillow, blasting music into the darkness.

Turner.

So he really did come, then?

I think about the implications of that and then shrug them off. Can't think about that right now. I can't even imagine what would happen if he decided to take all of his energy and focus it one me. I'd never escape. I grab my iPod and switch it off, flinging back the curtain and

checking to make sure I'm alone before I scramble out of bed and search for some clothes to throw on. I settle on a green Terre Haute tank, some acid washed jeans, and a pair of black heels. I have no clue what time it is right now, but since I didn't fall asleep until dawn, I can guess that the show isn't too far off. In the distance, I can hear the rumble and murmur of voices, the sounds of trailers being opened, equipment being dragged across the cement. Yep, it's just about that time.

I step into the bathroom and play with my hair, swirling it into a messy bun on the back of my head. A quick slash of eyeliner, some gray shadow and dark lipstick and I'm done. I like to look good, but I'm not a fussy chick. That's Hayden's role here.

I check around to make sure that she's gone and then jack a pair of her sunglasses. I doubt she'll even know I took them considering she's giving up the spotlight tonight to go take care of whatever it is she's so damn worried about. *I'm singing tonight.* I try to keep that thought out of my head, pretty damn certain that if I let it, it'll take hold of me and fuck me until I'm too nervous to even set foot on that stage. Being the center of attention isn't my thing either. That too, I leave to Hayden Lee. She thrives on that kind of shit. Me, not so much.

Dax and America are sitting at the table when I come out, but neither turns to look at me which is a bad sign.

They pretend like they're not watching which makes it all the more obvious that they are.

"Sorry about the late night conjugal visit," I say which makes America cringe and swivel to face me with clenched teeth. I pour myself a cup of coffee and drink it black, leaning against the counter and praying to god that I won't get any more plastic doll heads in the mail today.

"Yes, well. Hmm." That's all America says, but I can tell she's holding back. What she really wants to do is tear off that stupid red tie she's got on and leap at my face, claw my damn eyes out and tell me to stay the hell away from Turner Campbell. Instead, she just spins back to face Dax who still won't look at me. I feel like I should apologize for some reason, but I know how stupid that is. I don't owe him anything. He has a crush on me. So what? That's not my problem; that's his.

I finish my coffee and toss the mug in the sink, too riled up to sit still. Besides, there's so much going on, all I have to do is reach a hand into a hat and pull out a name. *Eric, Katie, Hayden, Turner.* If I don't start dismantling these mysteries, I'm going to drown in them.

Fortunately for me, one of them is waiting right outside the door.

"Hello, Eric," I say as I turn towards my former foster brother and admire the cream colored suit he's got on. The sharp cut of the shoulders and the perfect tailoring at

the waist tells me that this, too, is one expensive fucking coat he's got on.

"Naomi," he says, glancing around like he thinks the cops are lurking around the corner. I light up a cigarette and watch as he shifts his feet nervously. "Did you find them?"

"I told you I'd call if I did." I pause. "They were stolen."

Eric freezes for a moment and then nods, short and crisp, like this is all just a business transaction to him.

"Okay. So the police really do have them ... " He trails off and rubs at his perfectly shaved chin, gleaming like a damn baby's bottom it's so fucking smooth. "But why do they have my fingerprints on them and not yours?"

"Good question," I ask him as I move closer and grab the flask he's just removed with trembling hands from his pocket. "Why don't you ask it a little louder, so the whole camp can be sure to hear." Eric lets me shoo him away and over towards the same spot Turner and I were sitting last night. There are some teenagers nearby smoking pot, but we ignore them. They're already high as kites. "Have you heard anything from Katie?" I ask, wondering where that bitch is. She's really starting to get to me. If I let it, the paranoia could really become a problem.

"Nothing," he says with a sigh, adjusting his black tie and watching as I take a massive gulp of whatever it is he's got. Whiskey. Good whiskey this time. Nice. I hand it back. "But the police are still out looking for me." He sighs and sits down on the curb, burying his face in his hands. I watch unsympathetically. I mean, I feel bad for the guy, but if it comes down to me or him, he's the one that's going down. Call me cruel, but it's just survival. And his parents probably would've killed all three of us eventually, so in a sense, he owes me one. "I don't know what to do. Even if I find her, that won't change anything. Somehow, I got it into my head that if I brought Katie back, things would be different. They won't be though, will they?" I just shrug and keep smoking, glancing over my shoulder occasionally to stare at Indecency's bus. It's at least twice the size of ours and a hell of a lot nicer, and that's saying a lot because ours costs as much as a fucking house.

"You just have to fight through it. You know you're innocent, so tell the damn truth. They'll figure it out eventually." I think back to the massive amount of questioning I was subjected to after the murder. I'm still having a hard time believing I got away with it, figure there has to be some other reason, some freak accident or loophole or sloppy police work that messed things up on their end. I mean, I was *all* over that crime scene. Eric, too, for that matter. And even Hayden was there, watching from inside the Rhineback's closet. I swallow hard.

"Really? You really want me to do that? You'll be brought back in, too, you know." And he's right, and I do know, and I absolutely cannot go through that again. Eventually, they're going to catch me in a lie and I'm going to be fried. If I'd shot them in the head, nice and clean, kept the videos of them torturing Katie then maybe I'd be alright. But I didn't. I killed them by stabbing a pair of *scissors* into their throats. Police kind of frown on that sort of thing. It's so much harder to claim self-defense in a situation like that, but I wasn't thinking clearly. After I found the videos, saw so much worse being done first-hand. And then when they came after me, beat me till I bled, promised worse the next time. A person can only handle so much.

"Guess not," I say as he once again drops his head into his hands. A few seconds later, Eric's shoulders begin to shake and I guess that he's crying. *Pussy.* I didn't even cry after the abortion. Not before it either. I walked through those doors with a neutral face and stayed stoic for days after. God, I hate Turner. I hate him. Hate him. Hate him. Maybe if I repeat it enough, I'll be able to keep that emotion and that emotion only in my heart and ignore the other one that's been there since I

was sixteen years old, the one that refuses to die. It's hard to kill love, isn't it? Even false love. It's like a persistent weed, one that has to be pulled out by the root and burned. I sigh. "Well, at the very least, you could be a bit more careful. I saw your car idling last night by the exit. Like that wasn't fucking obvious."

Eric's eyes snap up to mine, a bright, piercing blue that cuts straight through me, reminding me of Katie and how she looked at me right before I left.

"And let me guess, that wasn't your car."

"It must've been Katie," Eric whispers, and I describe to him as best I can what the damn thing looked like. I realize as I start to do this that I need to be paying more attention. I can hardly remember anything other than the color. "Did you see where it went?" he asks me. "What direction?" I shake my head and Eric groans, letting his shoulders droop for a second before he perks up again. "If we checked the parking lot, do you think you could find it?" I shrug my shoulders, but I think I could, so I follow up with a nod.

"Yeah, sure, maybe."

"If I find her, maybe I can get her to confess to sending the scissors in and ... " Eric trails off, and I can see wheels turning inside his head.

"You're going to pin this on her?" I ask, feeling annoyed as fuck with this man. I can't believe I ever had

a crush on him, gave him my first kiss, let him hold my hand. I'm a terrible judge of men. Or I was. Now, I know better. Just like I know to stay clear of Turner Campbell. I need to start taking my own advice.

"What else do you want me to do, Naomi? It's either her or me, and we both know damn well that she's guilty."

I scrape the inside of my cheek with my teeth, using the sharpness of the pain to keep myself in check.

"I thought you wanted to protect her," I say nonchalantly, hoping he'll change his mind about this. I mean, pinning the murder on him is one thing. Pinning it on Katie, as crazy as she turned out to be, sort of defeats the whole purpose of my saving her in the first place. That girl's been locked up enough in her life. Yes, I'd prefer it if she'd stop sending videos of me murdering people to my acquaintances' phones, but I also don't want to see her in jail. I want her to live a nice, long, healthy, happy life far, far away from me.

"You don't know how bad it's gotten," he tells me, shaking his head like he can't come to terms with what's going on around him. "I had to have her committed."

"So you've said," I tell him as I fish out another cigarette. Eric takes a sip from his flask and stands up, letting his eyes slide over to the flow of traffic on the highway. I wonder, and not for the first time, where he

might've gotten that suit from. What business ventures does he have going on now? I almost don't want to know. I follow his gaze over to the cars and then back, glancing surreptitiously over at Indecency's bus, just to see if I can catch a glimpse of Turner. My lips purse and I end up getting angry with myself. "But you never bothered to give me any details. Like, what, she changed her hair to match mine? Her name? No, no, no, wait. She has a shrine dedicated to me in her bedroom with a dream catcher made of my hair. Is that it?"

Eric stands up without a word, letting the skin around the edges of his mouth wrinkle in disgust. When the moonlight hits his eyes just right, they reflect back at me.

"I didn't come here to be ridiculed, Naomi. I came here to ask for your help." He starts to walk away and then pauses to glance over his shoulder at me. "Oh, and if you see Katie, be careful. She might seem innocent, but looks are deceiving. You'd be surprised at what she's capable of."

About fifteen minutes before our set, America notices

that Hayden isn't around anymore. She was earlier which surprised me since I hadn't seen her all night. She popped in backstage and started bitching about something so inconsequential that I can't even remember what it was about. A few minutes later, right before Terre Haute took the stage, she said she was going outside to have a smoke and never came back in.

When America realizes this, she does what she does best and gets on her phone, making calls and texting Hayden. When that doesn't work, she sends me outside to look for her which, of course, is fruitless because Miss Lee is long gone by then.

I linger outside, just so she'll think I tried. If she doesn't believe I looked hard enough, she'll make me go back out again.

"Hey there, beautiful." I roll my eyes and turn to face a pair of twinkling brown eyes and an arrogant smirk.

"What do you want?" I ask Turner, doing my best to keep last night out of my mind and away from conscious thought. If I think about it, he'll know.

"To see how you were doing is all. That a crime?" I stare at him, taking in the tight black T-shirt he has plastered against his firm body, the ridiculous pants, the thick, leather boots. If he wasn't so attractive, this whole situation would be a lot easier to deal with.

"No, but breaking into someone's bus and fucking

them while they're in a drunken stupor is." Turner laughs, harsh and loud, and puts the brown beer bottle he's got clutched in his hand up to his lips.

"Oh come on," he says and then takes a sip. "You think I'm that fucking stupid? That I was born yesterday? I asked your friend, the one with the blonde hair and the blue fingernails to let me in. I figured since he's always sneaking onto my bus at night to screw my driver, that he might be willing to return the favor."

"So, let me get this straight. You, what, blackmailed Kash into letting you on the bus and then decided it was cool to fuck me while I was high?" Turner just stares at me and the arrogant expression on his face slips a bit, like he isn't quite sure what's going on. What did he expect? For me to throw myself into his arms and tell him what a stud he is? I mean, I'm not saying I didn't enjoy what happened between us last night, but let's be honest, it was a little weird. I keep that thought to myself and just stare him straight in the face.

"Seemed to me like you were enjoying yourself," he says, finishing his drink and tossing the bottle into the dumpster nearby. His full lips are starting to purse and he looks a little let down. Bad sign. I think about hitting him again just so he'll get pissed off, start swinging, go back to that volatile asshole he was a few days ago. Instead, he just clenches and unclenches his hands at his

sides.

"Yeah, well, there are some meth addicts out back, behind the fence near the highway. They're enjoying themselves, too. Doesn't mean it's good for them." The smallest hint of a smirk rides back up and onto Turner's face, causing his lip ring to catch the moonlight and reflect it into my face. I squint.

"So you're comparing me to meth, huh? Didn't know I was so addictive."

"Fuck you, Turner," I say, spinning around to grab the handle of the door. Before my fingers can wrap around the metal, he's touching me, sliding up close and grabbing me around the waist, pressing the heat of my body against his. My heart starts to pump and my hands begin to sweat. This is precisely the *last* thing I need before I hit the stage. When his lips brush my ear, my elbow goes back automatically and cracks him in the ribs.

A grunt escapes Turner's lips as he stumbles away and then looks up at me like I've lost my friggin' mind.

"What's your fucking problem?" he growls, letting his face wrinkle with anger. Finally. An emotion that I recognize. "You're hot then you're cold, like a fucking tap. What's the matter with you?"

"You," I tell him, pulling open the door a crack, so I can hear where Terre Haute is in their set. "And you have been for a long, long time. Why can't you just learn to

leave things well enough alone? We did our thing and now we're done. Stay away from me." I start inside and Turner follows, trailing behind me and reaching out to grab my wrist. I spin around and snatch it away from him. "Go away, Turner. I'm warning you." I know that Dax is probably watching us, America, too. I need to get rid of Turner now, so I can prepare myself to go onstage. This is going to be hard enough as it is.

"No," Turner says, stubborn as shit, staring at me like he's trying to pick me apart with his eyes. It'll never work. He couldn't figure me out if he tried. He doesn't know me, and he isn't going to. So what if he knows my secrets now? Who cares? He still did what he did to me, still is what he is, will never change. I can't even entertain the thought. The next words out of his mouth blow me away, break me up into little pieces, chew me up and spit me out. Holy fucking shit. "Let me give it to you straight, Naomi. I don't keep secrets. I hate them. They sit inside of you and they eat away at your fucking soul, so I'm just going to come right out with it." Turner pauses and takes a deep breath, face shadowed in the dimness, cheekbones highlighted by a stray sliver of light that's leaking from the stage. Vaguely, I hear America in the background asking about Hayden, but I don't care. Right now, all of my attention is focused on Turner Campbell and his narcissistic delusions. "I'm in love

with you."

Time stops, and I swear to God, I feel like my breath is being sucked out of me and swirled around the room, collecting energy from the space around me, so that when it all rushes back in, my chest is so tight that it feels like it's going to burst. I know that people are staring at us now, most of them just as shocked as I am, especially the girls. They've all probably fucked Turner, seen what an asshole he is, so they must know how weird this is for me. But they have no idea how much it hurts.

I reach up my hand to hit him, but he grabs my wrist and holds me back, keeping me at arm's length, so he can study my face and try to pick me apart. I hear applause from out front, and I know that it's almost time for me to go on and take Hayden's place, albeit temporarily, time for me to stand in the light when all I want to do is blend into the dark right now, hide my face and let these feelings wash over and through me.

"You selfish son of a bitch," I growl at him, yanking my wrist back with such force that I stumble. Behind me, Terre Haute exits the stage and equipment starts being shuffled around like pieces on a chess board. "I can't believe you even have the audacity to say that to my face." Turner looks confused as shit, like he doesn't understand why I'm not leaping into his arms and giving him my everything. Wow. I thought he was experienced,

but really, he's naive. He may have fucked a lot of girls, done a lot of drugs, had a hard life, but he knows nothing about love. Nothing at all. "You wouldn't know what love was if it bit you in the face, Turner." He narrows his eyes at me, frustrated that this isn't going the way he wanted. Well, fuck him. This is just the way it's going to be, the way it has to be. "Get this stupid idea out of your head and move the fuck on." I start to turn away, but he grabs onto my elbow and pulls me back, spinning me around so quick it makes my head spin. He lets go of me right away, but that doesn't stop Dax and Wren from grabbing him and pulling him back, holding him still while he tries to meet my eyes and explain something that he doesn't understand.

"I know that you're interesting to me, and you don't take my shit. I know that I remember you even though I shouldn't." Turner jerks his arms out of Dax's and Wren's grip, flicking himself in the side of the head for emphasis.

And fuck. There it is. There it fucking is, all of that passion and heat and intensity, focused right on me. I feel like Turner's just put a magnifying glass up to the sun and focused its rays down on my head. I feel dizzy and sick, and my ears are throbbing and America is screaming about Hayden. I start to shake violently.

"It's starting to come back to me, you know? Like, all the lurid fucking details." He stares at me hard, just locks

onto me and won't let go. "You gave me a blow job in an elevator, huh?" I close my eyes and count to ten. I'm not embarrassed. Why should I be? I just can't stand to listen to him recount that night right now, not before I go onstage and have all those eyes on me, focusing, judging. "Images have been flashing through my fucking brain of a night *six years ago* where I was so high, I don't even remember getting a tattoo." Turner points at me and growls, shaking his head like he can't even believe he has to say all this, like I should just be grateful he 'loves' me. Fuck him. "But I remember you. I didn't realize it at first, but I did." I do my best not to think about that night on the bus when he called me Naomi, and turn away like I don't care at all.

"I've gotta get ready to play," I tell him, but he isn't here to listen to fucking excuses. He keeps talking, but he doesn't move. He knows that if he does, the boys will be on him and he won't get even a step further.

"There are girls I fucked a week ago that I don't remember. I don't remember their names or what they looked like or what we did, only that there was a woman in my bed. And I'm sorry I didn't remember right away, and I'm sorry that I fucking left, but I'm here now. Fuck the past. The present's all that matters anyway, right?"

I spin back around so fast that my hair gets caught across my face and sticks to my lips. I take a few steps

towards Turner, getting so close to his face that when I talk, my mouth brushes his.

"Your past is your foundation, and if it's crumbling, then you've got nothing left to build on." I breathe out and Turner breathes in, exact opposites. "To start over, you have to create something new, somewhere strong and stable and sturdy or the whole thing will come crumbling down. And Turner, I can't pick up a piece of that old, rotted, fucking wood and make a new house with it, now can I? You had your chance with me. You're done. We're done. Leave me alone."

"Not a fucking chance," he tells me, breathes out; I breathe in. Our breath mingles in the hot air for another second before America steps between us, pushing us apart with strong arms and flat lips. It's only then I notice that they're ready for us onstage. Shit.

"I'm going to ask you one more time: where is Hayden?"

"She's not coming," I spit, turning away, looking around at the rest of the band. They don't look nervous though, just confused. "I'll be filling in for her."

"Oh? Will you?" America asks, laughing like a hyena on the fucking plains. She sounds like she's ready for blood. "She have somewhere better to be?"

"Apparently," I respond, refusing to look at Turner's face. My lungs are full of him now though, and I swear

that even with all the noise around me, I can still hear him breathing.

America doesn't respond, but the skin on her cheeks and forehead is so tight it looks like she just got a face-lift or something. I look away from her and out at the bit of the crowd I can see from here, buzzing and murmuring, waiting for Turner probably. That's why most of them are here, to see him before Indecency's new record deal goes through and they become untouchable, playing venues so big that a football stadium looks small.

Without another word, I step forward and leave the drama behind, moving with stiff confidence over to my guitar. I slide the strap over my head and step up to the center mic. Okay, so I won't be able to put on the sexed up show they're looking for, but I can blow their mind with music. That's what I have to do right now, for them and for me. I glance over to my left as the rest of the band files out behind me and catch Turner's eye.

He's mad, yeah, but determined. Getting away from him is going to be damn near impossible.

I turn back to face the crowd and take a deep breath, doing my best to pull that inner me out, so she can take over. I can't slide into myself right now or this whole night's going to be for shit. A bad show on top of a bad day will only make things worse. I have to rule this. I'm a fucking rock star, after all, aren't I?

"Hey there." I pause for a moment and try to remember where the fuck it is we're at. "Colorado." Some cheers go up but not enough. I see people glancing at one another, disappointed, and once that happens, I start to pick the crowd apart, take the image of these people in my head from a single entity to thousands of tiny dots with frowns and sneers and laughter. I let my eyes shutter briefly for a moment. *Get ahold of yourself. You're a strong woman. You going to let a little stage fright fuck you up?* I open my eyes and sweep the dark mass below me. It stretches out and back, spreading out on either side and tapering off at roped entry points beyond which tables sit, covered in drinks, surrounded by even more people. My throat goes dry, and I find myself having trouble speaking. I open my mouth again and nothing will come out. I blame Turner. This is his fault. I could've handled this. After all, it's not like it's my first time onstage. He just tightened that noose around my neck, and I feel like I'm being choked. Do you know how hard it is to be offered the one thing you always wanted just after you've convinced yourself that you don't anymore? Just when you've accepted that you'll never have it? It's cruel. Worse than never being offered it at all.

"How's it fucking going, Denver?"

Turner's got Wren's mic in his hand and is strolling

towards me with a smirk on his face, one that betrays the glint of anger and hope that's warring in his eyes.

"You know Naomi Knox, right?" he asks, and he holds his hand over my head, starting the crowd up like a revving engine, just a slight purr that you know will become a rumble before long. "You're going to have to forgive her. Her leading lady, Miss Anorexia herself … " A murmur of laughter ripples through the group. "Is MIA at the moment, so tonight, you're going to get the extreme pleasure," he purrs as he drops his hand and rubs his belly, purposing exposing the taut flesh above his jeans. "Of listening to her sing. I just announced my undying love for her, so she's a little flustered at the moment. I'm sure once she realizes she feels the same way, she'll calm down." More laughter, a little nervous this time but quite a bit louder, bursts from the group, and then the crowd starts a chant. *Duet. Duet. Duet.* They want Turner and I to sing together. Of course they do. They've all seen that video of us on YouTube.

I purse my lips tight and glance at him from the corner of my eye. God, he looks like an angel again, highlighted under the bright lights, blue-black hair gleaming, tattoos vibrant and popping. I don't want to do this with him, but I don't know how to get rid of him either. A rock and a hard place. Guess I just have to figure out how to make that *hard rock* and we're good to go.

Turner turns to face me, still smirking, still looking arrogant as fuck in the mouth but dangerously unstable in the eyes. What a volatile place to be. I swallow hard and strike a chord. We start up *Turning the Key on the Past,* totally fucking up our setlist for the night. Oh well. Fuck it. I need to play this song. Turner needs to hear it. He was right; it's about him anyway.

I press my lips to the mic and try not to think too hard about this. Either he'll join me or he won't. I don't care.

My voice, when I start to sing, sounds loud, too loud, and lonely. I sound good, I think, but not quite right.

"Struggling to understand why this pain feels different from what I've felt before."

When Turner's voice cuts in through the other mic, I falter and I miss the next line entirely, wrapped up in the golden chords of his voice that curl so tightly around me that I forget to breathe for a second and end up lightheaded and dizzy.

"Waking up to the sound of your voice, playing in my head, always running in my head."

When he exhales at the end of the line, I inhale and start up again. This time, both of our voices join together and mine doesn't sound so lonely anymore. The stage vibrates with sound as Wren and I destroy it with our guitars, pulling Blair and Jesse and Dax along for the ride. The crowd is screaming now, having an absolute

panic attack and rushing forward, crushing the poor people in the front against the bars so tightly that the bouncers have to rescue them and pull them over, escorting them to the edges to watch with wide eyes and heaving chests.

"*When I walk, I stumble. When I run, I fall. 'Cause it's the same mistake that will fool us all. I fell in love. I ... I fell in love. I. Fell. In. LOVE!*"

Turner curls over with that last scream, folding down and then bouncing back up, spinning in a circle and thrashing his head back down. If I thought things were intense before, I was wrong. That was just a tease. *This is gonna get worse before it gets better, isn't it?* My pulse starts to pick up, moving at a dangerous speed, so quick I can feel it throbbing against the side of my throat.

"*And we, we just can't be. There is no place to go where the pain won't find us.*" Turner leans into me and puts his face close, too close. Unconsciously, I wet my lips with my tongue, and the rest of the band picks up the next verse while Turner and I dance around each other, spinning in a slow circle, stomping the stage beneath our feet with each step.

"*Because we're the broken ones, the halves that got left behind, the hearts that will never stop bleeding. We fell in love. We ... we fell in love, and only you fell out of it.*"

My hands comes down hard, hits the strings and vibrations travel through me, take over my brain and close the door on my inhibitions. The inner me is hanging all the way out, kicking around like a fucking maniac, like I've just freaking lost it and gone crazy. It was only a matter of time anyway. See, this is why I didn't want a confession of love. This shit is just … it's insane.

And then it all stops and there's this freakish bit of quiet before Blair starts in on her keyboard solo, fingers flying over her instrument like she's casting a spell, a rock goddess bitch witch of fucking insanity. Turner takes advantage of this moment to step behind me and slide his arms over my shoulders. An unwanted moan breaks its way out of my throat just as Turner lifts the mic to my mouth. My own sound echoes through the crowd, amplified and shocking in its nakedness. I want to throw him off, but I'm busy with my guitar, plucking strings with my pick again, being the leader that I've always been, just without knowing it. Hayden is a front, that's all, like a figurehead. Can't believe it took me this long to figure out that I was in charge.

"Why are you being so stubborn?" Turner whispers into my ear, nibbling it with his teeth while a thousand plus strangers look on. "Just give me a chance."

"And we just can't be, and there's no place to go, and

the pain will always find us." Turner lets me sing the line by myself, moving one of his hands up and over my breasts before he spins away and swings the mic like he's in an old-timey fucking radio. "*Because of love, all because of love.*"

Sweat is pouring down my face, too much for just the venue and the press of people and the movement. In fact, I think it has more to do with what's going on inside of me than what's going on out. I get tongue-tied again, unused to the dual pressures of singing and playing at the same time. Turner saves me again, but I have to wonder if, like our very first meeting, he's saving me so he can screw me later, leave me worse off than before.

"*Faceless faces and barren voices can't pull me out because I'm in too deep, and my love is killing me. If I don't turn a key on my past, oh, my fucking past, then I'll never make it out alive.*"

My guitar solo comes up hard and my mind seriously goes fucking blank. I feel like I'm high, only I'm not. I swear that my hands aren't my own as I finger my Wolfgang, fucking it with demonic strokes and tearing the venue down, brick by fucking brick.

Turner's breath hits my neck again as I finish and hit my guitar, spinning it around my back and to the front again. Screams go up, and the energy increases to a point where it's almost painful. When this happens, it feels like

I'm possessed, like I can't make any decisions on my own. It's all the music, has always been the music, because it's a reflection of the soul. And the soul knows best. After all, it's powered by the most powerful thing there is: the heart.

Turner kisses me, and I know it's wrong, and I know I should stop, but instead I let my tongue slide into his mouth, swirl up the heat and the pain and the energy, pulling away only when I have to to finish the song. Between verses, we find each other again, his hands on my neck, his fingers in my hair. We even let the rest of the band pick up the chorus. All the while, I continue to play, my knuckles brushing the erection in Turner's pants, strumming him at the same time I strum my guitar. It's so ridiculous, and I just know I'm going to hate myself later for this, but I can't stop. Until this song is over, I belong to the music. We all do.

A crescendo builds outside and in, and my clit throbs and pulses. My thighs are wet with sweat and lube, sliding together as I jam hard, drawing in the crowd for a collective breath that they'll hold until I damn well say otherwise. Just when they think they're going to burst, that they're going to die if they don't exhale, Turner and I break apart and scream the last words to the song, voices so loud and strained that they break on the last syllable.

The song ends; he steps away from me; I smash my

guitar to pieces on the stage and chuck what's left of it into the greedy hands of the crowd.

CHAPTER 26
TURNER CAMPBELL

My emotions are so fucking raw right now that I can't seem to stay in control of myself. I just keep doing shit without thinking it through. My body is pulsing and vibrating, being plucked by the dirty hands of fate. As soon as I get offstage, I start to pace, running my fingers through my hair and doing my best not to think about Travis's hat. It was a prank. Had to be. None of the guys will admit to it, but obviously somebody's trying to fuck with us. I think of Naomi's foster sister, but have no clue how she'd have even known what type of hat Travis wore. I mean, the cap couldn't have been one of the ones he'd *actually* worn, but it was the same style – black with a white brim, eagle with outstretched wings on the back. I mean, if it's a coincidence, it's an eerie one.

I brush Milo off, not really in the mood to hear him bitch, and watch as Naomi is outfitted with a backup guitar. She starts the next song off with a shaking voice but quickly pulls up her strength and pushes through the skull of the crowd, bending them to her will, marking that whole place with her power and her voice.

I want her so bad right now that it hurts. Literally. My dick is smashed up inside my pants, grinding against the denim, and my hands are clenched so tight that my knuckles are straining against my skin. I stalk back and forth and wait, keeping my eyes off of her sweaty body.

I confessed my love to her.

I cannot even believe that shit. I blame it on the conversation I had with Ronnie, the shock of finding the baseball cap. She didn't exactly react positively to the news, but then, onstage, she was all the fuck over me.

I grab a white towel and throw it around my neck, using the end to wipe the sweat from my forehead and end up stealing a beer from one of the roadies, finishing it in one gulp. No wonder I've never bothered to fall in love before. It sucks. Love sucks. It sucks big, fat, hairy fucking dick. My bandmates watch me pace like a tiger in a cage, but everybody keeps their mouths shut tight. Good thing, too, because I'm wound up so tight that anything could set me off.

Testosterone and adrenaline mix in my blood, creating this toxic concoction that has me on edge through Amatory Riot's entire set. It's so bad that I can't even look at them play. All I can do is stand there and close my eyes, let my head fall back and my hands shake. Naomi's voice is crazy fucking good, so much better than Skinny Chick's. I wonder briefly where that bitch is anyway, but figure it isn't all that important.

As soon as Naomi walks offstage, I go after her.

"Don't touch me," she whispers, voice low and gravelly. She's growling at me for fuck's sake, and it's *hot*. All eyes are on us as we move towards the back door like a storm cloud, bouncing energy off of one another's skin. I'm so hypersensitive right now that I'm having a really, really hard time forming logical thoughts in my brain. I can see every bead of sweat on her skin, her dilated pupils, her taut nipples. "Stay away from me." Naomi pauses with her fingers on the handle of the door, and it's almost like I can hear the entire room taking a breath, holding it, waiting to see what's going to happen between us. "I don't love you."

"You will." Maybe that's the wrong thing to say, but it comes out of my mouth anyway. I'm not used to not getting my way. I might be overcompensating for my shitty childhood, but that's just the way it is. I want, no I *need*, Naomi to respect me. Somehow, her opinion is the

only one that's important right now. But of course she doesn't love me, not yet. "You hate me. I get it. I can wait."

"Goddamn it, Turner!" she shouts, punching the door so hard that her knuckles come back bloody. She turns on me and her eyes are wild, not just wet but soaked, drenched. They don't even look brown now, just orange, bright as the fucking sun. "You're right. I do." She points at me with one of her silver painted fingernails. "You're a cocky, arrogant, self-serving, smug, selfish piece of shit. You don't love me. You just think you do. You're interested in me because you can't have me." She throws her arm out to indicate the rest of the room. "You could have almost any girl here or out there or anywhere, anyone that's single and available and a lot that aren't. You like me because I'm a challenge, but as soon as the challenge is over and you've won, you'll get bored and you'll wander." Naomi sucks in a massive breath and steps close to me, brushing the toes of my shoes with hers. "To love something or someone, you have to be willing to give up everything else you care about to make things right for them, even if the decision is hard or it sucks or it makes you so miserable you want to tear your teeth out of your fucking skull." She looks me straight in the eye and holds me there with that piercing gaze. "You're not there yet, Turner. You're just not, and that's

pretty obvious, even to me, and I'm no fucking expert." Naomi touches her fingers to the bleeding heart tattoo on her chest. "Life is real, and it's ugly, and it hurts. I've only ever loved three things in my life, and none of them worked out for me."

I stand there in silence and listen to her speech with my cock throbbing and my heart pounding. Sweat is pouring down my face and into my eyes, and my breath is coming fast and shallow, making my vision spotty and blurry. I'm jealous, I admit. Stupid as it fucking sounds, even after her impressive but admittedly hurtful speech, I can only think about one thing.

"What are they?" She stares at me like I'm the craziest person she's ever laid eyes on. Her laugh, when it does come, is harsh and painful.

"God, you're a fucking idiot." Naomi holds up three fingers. I can't help but notice that they're shaking, too. "You." She drops one finger against her palm, and I take a step forward, letting flashes of memory flicker over the top of my vision. I can remember her telling me that before, but I didn't get it. I've had lots of girls tell me that in bed. It's just something people say. Honestly, I think she's the only one that ever meant it. "Your baby." Naomi drops her second finger, leaving only her middle up, so she can flip me the bird. "But I could not, in good conscious, force her to suffer alongside the rest of us."

She pauses and takes a deep breath. "And myself. I lost that love a long, long time ago, and I'm only now just starting to get that back. I won't let you take it from me." She pauses and lets her hand fall to her side, shifting her eyes away from mine. She doesn't stop shaking.

"I wouldn't dare," I tell her, trying to get her to look at me, but she won't. She flat out refuses to give me the satisfaction. "And I could probably teach you a thing or two about it. If anyone's an expert in loving themselves, it's me." It's a joke ... sort of. But Naomi doesn't laugh. Instead, the words hang in the air like they've been drawn there, etched into the white smoke that drifts lazily around the room. Part of me is aware that I've got to get onstage soon. The rest of me doesn't care. I stand very, very still, and I wait. After what seems like forever, Naomi drops her hand and licks her lips.

"If you're waiting for a declaration of love from me, it isn't coming." She looks at me and then glances over her shoulder at the bits of broken guitar that were salvaged off the stage and placed inside of a plastic bag. Her manager's holding them now, and she doesn't look all that happy about it. I try to stick to my honesty policy. I figure I sound like a dick anyway, so I may as well just go for it. If you've got nothing to hide, it's a hell of a lot harder for other people to hurt you.

"Nah, baby, right now, I just kind of want to fuck." If

I don't touch her before I go onstage, I'm going to be worse than animalistic. It'll get real ugly, real fast. Sex, drugs, and rock 'n' roll, right? Fucking toxic. Still, I think she's wrong about me. I know love because I know the absence of it, you know what I mean? Like, I know black because I've seen white, something like that. But just telling that to Naomi isn't going to do me shit. I'm going to have to prove it a thousand times over. There's a lot of baggage that has to be dealt with first.

She looks at me with an expressionless mask plastered over her face, then back at her band, then at the door. After a moment, she reaches down and touches her fingertips to the handle. I can tell she wants me just as badly as I want her. When we're onstage together, we just connect. We're like *this*.

"I don't think that's such a good idea right now," she whispers, and I hear this whoosh of air, like everybody that's been watching us can finally breathe again. The silence breaks, and the roar of the crowd comes echoing violently out at me. *Duet. Duet. Duet.* They want Naomi back. Can't say I blame 'em.

"Encore?" I ask her, but my heart is sinking fast, drowning in blood. I feel like I'm sweating excitement out through my pores. I feel like something is happening, but instead of an explosion, it's a whisper. It happens so quietly and discreetly that I hardly notice it. I'm not used

to subtlety anymore. I've been living with everything happening in a big way for so long that I miss it. That's my fucking problem. Since there's nothing crashing down around me, I don't notice that anything's wrong.

I should have never let her walk out that door.

"Turner," she says as pulls the handle down and steps forward. "Fuck off."

As soon as she leaves, I have a mild freak out and punch the wall so hard that my entire arm goes numb for a moment. If I didn't have a fucking show to do, I'd chase after her. I think she knows that. By the time I get out there, it's going to be too late. The night's fucking ruined. *But there's always tomorrow, right?* Unfortunately, that's not always true, but I guess I don't realize that yet.

When the crowd starts to chant my name, I snarl deep in my throat and storm that stage, ready to fucking destroy them. They're going to get their money's worth tonight, that's for fucking sure. I lost the battle with Naomi, but I'm going to win the war. Eventually.

After all, Turner Campbell always gets what he wants.

By the time we're finished with our set, I'm ready to go on a rampage, storming off into the night with a cigarette between my lips and Milo shouting at my back. He's saying something a record exec and a deal, and I just don't fucking care right now. If he wants me, he'll wait. I'm not begging anything from anyone anymore. I figure, if they really want to sign us, they'll stick around. At the moment, I'm nursing the world's worst hard-on, rubbed raw against my jeans and aching like a fucking bitch. I just want to go back to the bus, snort a few lines and take a fucking shower. I don't even want to touch myself.

All I can think about is Naomi, like an all consuming fire, she's taken hold of me and turned everything else to ash. Jesus Christ. I run trembling fingers through my hair. If I'm this bad now, what happens next week? Or next month? Am I going to get progressively worse? I don't know shit about how this works, and there's nobody that I'm willing to ask about it. Anyway, the only person I can even think of who's been in love is Ronnie, and he's the last one I'd ever talk to. Whenever Asuka's name comes up in conversation, he just loses it.

So I pace outside for awhile, just to burn some energy, when I notice this girl staring at me from the edge of the fence. It's kind of obvious that she's just jumped it, making me pretty damn sure that when I actually find my fucking bodyguard, that I'm going to fire him.

She's looking at me with big, blue eyes, haunted eyes, eyes that tell a story I don't want to hear. Her blonde hair is buzzed short, military style, so close to her skull that she almost looks bald at first. She's got on a white dress that's stained with dirt and in her hands is a purse, clutched so tight it looks like her fingers are going to snap off. Something about her catches my attention and not in a good way. When this girl walks, angels cry. That's how sad she is. Something bad happened to her, and it's written all over her face. As she starts to walk towards me, I change my mind. Not something. A whole lot of fucking somethings. Jesus, Mary, and fuck.

"Am I too late?" she asks me, biting her lip and glancing around surreptitiously, like she expects something horrible to crawl out of the darkness at the edge of the lot and consume her, flesh, blood, and bones. "Is she still here?"

I take my cigarette out of my mouth and toss it to the ground at my feet.

"She?" I ask as the girl moves tentatively towards me. She's kind of freaking me out, to be honest. I glance over my shoulder and see Treyjan storming across the lot. He wants to rip me a new one for what happened backstage, but fuck him. This is nobody's business but mine anyway. If I want to fall in love, that's my problem, not his. I really don't want to deal with his shit tonight, but at

least if this girl turns out to be a crazed fan, I'll have someone at my back. Can't ask for anyone better in a fight.

"Naomi," she whispers, and then it just clicks. The foster sister. Fuck. I take a step backward, but the girl is already shaking her head. "I don't know what he told you, but whatever it is, it's a lie." She pauses and bites at her lip, like a rat trying to chew its way through the bars of a cage. It's disturbing as shit. "This is big, much bigger than I first thought." She stares at me, and I find myself unable to look away. I let my hands roam down to my pockets for another cigarette. "Much bigger than you and me."

"Who the fuck are you?" I ask her as she continues forward, brow scrunching up so tight that her forehead looks like it has ripples.

"Where's Naomi?" The girl pauses and squeezes her eyes shut tight. "Please tell me she's still here, that I'm not too late. Please. Please. Please."

"What the fuck are you even talking about?" I ask, contemplating what the fuck it is that I should do. Do I call the cops? Do I get Naomi? Is it safe to show this chick where she is? "Naomi's back at her bus, I guess."

"When's the last you saw her?" the girl asks, leaning forward and staring unblinking up at me. I think that's about the moment when I first hear the sirens. Both the

girl and I turn to look. "Oh no," she whispers, and then she starts running. Not away like I think at first, but towards the sounds, towards the red and blue lights that are swinging in off the highway.

The cigarette falls from my fingers. My heart stops beating. I don't know when it hits me, but when it does, I start running, too.

"Fuck."

Naomi.

That's where the sirens are headed. And it's not just police. Just police I can handle. But there's an ambulance. No, no, no … *two* ambulances. I run faster and manage to outpace the blonde girl who's running with tears streaming down her face. It's only then that I realize she's barefoot.

I hit the stairs to the bus first, before the girl, before the cops and the EMS workers.

Dax is already there, and he tries to stop me, holds out his arm and catches me before I slip in it.

Bile rises in my throat and my head begins to spin.

The entire room is coated in blood. It's everywhere: floors, walls, even the ceiling. It's splattered everywhere, just everywhere, all over fucking everything. My eyes are wide now, and my heart is beating so loud I can hear it in my skull.

"Don't look, just don't look at it," Dax is shouting,

tears streaming down his face. The world goes silent. There are two bodies on the floor, two female bodies, naked, bloody, beaten, blonde. Either of them could be Naomi. Neither of them could. A line of a song slides through my skull.

To find you, only to lose you, even the devil couldn't think up a hell worse than that. I abused you, when I should've held you, and only the truth will set us free.

I turn to my right and vomit, all over the back of the captain's chair. The barefoot girl climbs the steps behind me and stands with her hand on the railing and her chin lifted in the air.

"I knew it," she whispers. "He got here first."

And then there are men in uniform, dragging me and Dax and the girl back, pulling us out of the blood, away from the scent of copper and pain. My first instinct is to fight, and I end up elbowing a cop in the face. They cuff me and throw me in the back of a squad car, but I still have a first row seat to what's going on in front of me.

One body goes on a stretcher, the other in a body bag. I don't know which is which, and it's killing me.

This can't be happening. It just can't. I can't discover Naomi only to lose her. How fucked up is that? And she can't be dead, not yet, not with that pain she's carrying around. She deserves someone to show her a good time first, show her that life isn't all bad. Maybe I'm not the

one, but maybe I am. How the fuck are either of us supposed to know, to be happy? If she is gone, I get the feeling that I am really and truly screwed. And I also know that I don't care because without her on this earth, nothing else will matter. Not even me.

Blue and red lights flash as the ambulances speed away. Well, one speeds, one goes slow. That's the one that scares the shit out of me. I drop my head to the back of the seat, and I scream. It echoes out the open window and ricochets around the lot.

In the midst of the gathering crowd around me, somebody smiles.

TO BE CONTINUED...

Dear Reader,

I want to apologize for the cliff-hanger. It's super screwed up, and I'm sorry. Unfortunately, not everything gets to be tied up in a pretty bow, especially not a story as fucked up as this. What I can promise you is that you'll get an ending ... eventually. Check for the second book in the series, coming soon. It's a real doozy, but I promise you answers.

Peace and love.
C.M.

P.S. Thanks for reading! I hope you enjoyed the story, and I look forward to sharing the rest of this journey with you. Readers imbue words with magic, and I can't thank you enough for that.

<3

About the Author

C.M. Stunich was raised under a cover of fog in the area known simply as Eureka, CA. A mysterious place, this strange, arboreal land nursed Caitlin's (yes, that's her name!) desire to write strange fiction novels about wicked monsters, magical trains, and Nemean Lions (Google it!). She currently enjoys drag queens, having too many cats, and tribal bellydance.

She can be reached at author@cmstunich.com, and loves to hear from her readers. Ms. Stunich also wrote this biography and has no idea why she decided to refer to herself in the third person.

Happy reading and carpe diem!

www.cmstunich.com

28675912R00177

Printed in Great Britain
by Amazon